The Graphologist's Apprentice

The Graphologist's Apprentice

Whiti Hereaka

First published in 2010 by Huia Publishers
39 Pipitea Street, PO Box 17–335
Wellington, Aotearoa New Zealand
www.huia.co.nz

ISBN 978-1-86969-422-7

Copyright © Whiti Hereaka 2010
Cover design/illustration: Three Eyes Ltd

All rights reserved. No part of this publication may be reproduced, stored in a retrieval system, or transmitted in any form or by any means, electronic, mechanical, including photocopying, recording or otherwise, without prior permission of the publisher.

National Library of New Zealand Cataloguing-in-Publication Data
Hereaka, Whiti.
The graphologist's apprentice / Whiti Hereaka.
ISBN 978-1-869694-22-7
1. New Zealand fiction— 21st century. I. Title.
NZ823.3—dc 22

Published with the assistance of

To Cam

One

Grey, grey, grey; the sky, the city, the hour. Today the wind is the kind that sucker punches you, stealing the breath from your lungs and making you feel, well, winded. It is the kind of wind that cyclones around your body, binding your clothes to your legs, halving each step you take. It is the kind of wind that knots your hair.

January has lived here just shy of a decade but she has learnt the ways of the wind; how to walk when nature is intent on pushing you back, that rain can fall sideways instead of on the ground, that the combination of lip gloss and hair paint your face with stripes in the slightest breeze.

She is a black sail in the wind; her long skirt flies behind her and her hair whips her in the face. Her pace is slow despite her rush; another morning, another alarm slept through. If she rushed now what kind of precedent would that create? They might expect her at the office on time every morning. January rubs her eyes, forgetting the black eyeliner encircling them. Now at least her tiredness looks like a sartorial decision; a carefully thought-out look to make her green eyes pop against her olive skin.

The street almost deserted an hour ago has filled with people and cars all rushing past the beautiful old houses that slowly turn into the shiny buildings that the eighties left behind. Signs advertising the latest apartment development scream – on-site gym, competitive prices, investors take notice! The buildings are sterile; too new to have any kind of character. In certain lights, if you squint, they are like giant filing cabinets; tidying people away stacked neatly on top of one another. On one balcony a terracotta pot filled with the remnants of a once living plant; the soil dried out by the wind. A small-town girl at heart, January wants a lawn, a piece of green to sit on and tend. She doesn't care if it is only big enough to lay a beach towel down. An impossible dream. She will be renting for the rest of her life. Yet she knows if she ever gets the money together for a deposit that this is what she could afford. Hell, not even these. She'd be lucky if she could afford a studio, the kind that real estate agents euphemistically call 'cosy' or 'open plan living'. The apartment buildings are jagged teeth in a smile that taunts her – 'You can't aspire to anything greater than me!'

It is no coincidence that she still lives by the university. For one, she can afford the rent and she can walk to work. But what really anchors her there has nothing to do with pragmatism. Something inside her doesn't want to let go. When she was studying the world was portioned out in semesters and exams; each class was an item on a list to be ticked off. She knew exactly what she wanted because she chose it from the calendar every new year. Success was black and white – a pass or a fail grade – not the undefined, murky depths of 'self-satisfaction'. What does that even mean; money, a spouse, a job? Somehow January has spent four years in her tide-me-over-until-my-career-starts job. In the beginning she still believed that she would find something better, something fulfilling, and she'd apply for anything. But one by one the rejection letters came, closing off each aspiration, making the next application that much harder to send, until eventually she gave up on leaving all together. Besides, it is easier to bitch and moan about your life than to do anything about it.

January walks to exorcise her of these thoughts. Every day she bundles them up and sets them free on the wind. Somehow they always find a way back.

BEEP! BEEP!

The driver honks and yells at the pedestrians that have thwarted his attempt to run the red. January's heartbeat is as scattered as the rest of the flock the ugliest car in the world almost mowed down. She can't control the giggle. The pedestrians bubble around his car like he is a piece of ice in a glass of lemonade. Except he's lost his cool; stuck in the middle of the intersection. Drivers like that ought to be branded, at least for public safety. He must know it too; why else would he buy a boxy old tank painted safety orange? When he gets his green, January waves to him; his snarl folds the rest of her fingers to her palm, her hand twists and her middle finger continues its lazy arc.

The rush of elation at being alive is dissipated by the reality that she is alive here. January feels queasy; she should have called in sick but she's taken so many days off lately that there would have been questions. Her feet suddenly turn to concrete as she trudges toward her office, the feeling of drowning in the grey of the city slowly filling her mouth and nose. She will emerge from here five days from now, grey and lifeless, and she'll undergo a two-day resurrection before she is thrown in again. It's not fair. Jesus had three days. January steps inside her building. She gulps a breath and holds it; clinging to life as work drags her down to oblivion.

'Oh look. It's our least favourite month. Late as usual.'

The Anorexia Twins. They lord over reception, eye candy, probably hired by the manager as a testimony to his own inadequacies. Thoroughbred, their bloodstock destined for some rich man, as a trophy. They stick together and are never seen apart.

Which is a good thing, because combined they almost make a whole person.

A1, as January likes to think of her, palomino skin against bright white hair. Startling blue eyes peer out under long black lashes, her teeth bright as pearls against her permatan.

A2, a glossy brunette, fine-featured and skittish, her deep brown eyes veiled with impossibly long dark lashes. January got the feeling that she would take flight if stared at head-on.

They watch January as she approaches. January suddenly feels like she ought to have brought an apple or a lump of sugar to appease them.

'It has been unusually warm for May ...'

'What are you talking about, you weirdo?'

January suddenly feels apologetic for her existence. 'Um, the weather?'

It has taken ten years for January to finally understand her high school drama teacher's favourite monologue:

Will you hyenas shut up! There is no sound on this earth that is worse than girlish giggling! None!

It is worse when it is directed at you.

January is riveted to the floor, afraid if she moves that they might bolt and stampede; crushing her beneath their spiked stillettos. The acid of their laughter leeches away and the tone becomes lighter, sweeter. The twins sit up, pulling their shoulders back to make the most of what their surgeon gave them. January knows that this is not for her benefit, and turns to see a courier behind her.

'Hey ladies, I've got a package for you.'

The twins bray on cue. He gives January a wink and she slinks away while the twins are distracted.

January has managed to sneak undetected all the way to her desk, keeping her head low past the cubicle walls. It is her computer that gives her away, greeting her like an over-enthusiastic puppy when she turns it on.

'Morning Jan. You should probably mute that …'

'You say that every day, Alice.'

'And you never listen to me. So what happened this morning?'

'I was almost killed.'

'Really?' Alice purrs the first syllable; stretching it out. 'Like the time you thought you had Legionnaires'?'

'The water tasted funny. But this time I really did …'

'Almost die?'

'And before I had my coffee too.' January drops her head to her desk with a heavy groan. 'How did it happen, Alice? How did we get stuck in a job like this?'

'We were lifed.'

'That's not even a word …'

'This job provides us with the means to nurture ourselves physically; a roof over our heads and food to eat. But it doesn't do anything more than that. The fantasy that there is a career out there that meets your every need is just a fantasy. You just have to stop defining your life by your job, January. It can't possibly fulfil your needs on a spiritual level. You need to find something else to fulfil your life.'

Great, something else to search for. It's hard enough to find a cute pair of shoes in this town, never mind a great purpose.

'Here, this will make you feel better.'

January cannot lift her head under the weight of Monday and mortality. Her desk is cool and slightly sticky against her cheek. Two cups of coffee slide into view.

Is she offering me Chairman Meow?

The Chairman Meow mug was a special Christmas gift. Alice's mother had had a picture of Alice's precious cat, the aforementioned Meow, printed on it. January had thought of two things when she first saw it. Firstly, who knew you could get your cat printed on a mug? Secondly, who would get a picture of their cat printed on a mug? Since the moment she opened the gift Alice has been obsessed with her mug: even more so now that Chairman Meow is past his glorious party days and his fur is matted and dull. On the mug he sits up proudly, his fur gleaming; ceramic perfect glaze. Alice hates anyone touching her mug.

Everyone else in the office uses the brown glass Arcoroc mugs that have been scratched to death by the dishwasher. Alice's mug has never seen the dishwasher. It is carefully hand washed by Alice, hunched over it protectively like a person trying to hide their PIN at an ATM. The only time it leaves her desk is to be filled with coffee or to be washed. It sits in its own groove on Alice's desk, created by coffee ring after coffee ring melting the perfect hole just to the right of her keyboard. January often marvels at the way Alice can bring it to her lips and place it down precisely, not a millimetre off, back into its position fifteen centimetres diagonally from the shift key. It is like there is something that draws it to the spot, like it is meant to be there, and for the past few years it has been.

January's hand hovers over Meow: the devil inside her wants to take it and see what Alice would do – would she stand by and watch as another pressed her lips against it, feeling the infidelity as keenly as if it were her spouse? Would January enjoy Alice's jealous squirm as she drank deeply from the cup, her lips plump and wet from the heat of the coffee? Is she really that cruel?

Perhaps she will never know. Chairman Meow disappears from view and nestles safely in his owner's plump hands. January lifts her head slightly to take a sip of coffee. It takes a while to hit her system, but when it does the caffeine jolts a memory free. She should thank Alice, that's what people do. She straightens her back and prepares herself. Short and sincere is all that is needed. Just look her in the eye and say ... but as January lifts her head she registers the full horror of the situation. She tries to look away, but her eyes are riveted and she cannot.

'You've done something to your hair,' is all she can manage.

'Yeah, I had it done this weekend. You like it?'

January is no stranger to hair disasters herself, having spent the late nineties sporting the Wellington fringe, an over-short thick fringe that made her look like she had a mono-brow. Women all over the city fell prey to this evil haircut: they would look at each other with sympathy as the fringe would puff up in the wind because it did not have enough weight to stay down. Their fringes would be shiny with sticky product to coax the hair to lie straight, gluing it to their foreheads. The worst part was when they had had enough and tried to grow the damn thing out. January decided to lop all her hair off rather than suffer through the indignity of looking like an electrified poodle. She unconsciously touches her long, dark hair and promises never to do that again, shuddering at the memory.

Yes, January had borne witness to hair disasters in her day. But Alice's hair was in a category of its own, off the Richter scale.

'It's like ...'

It reminds January of vegemite and crackers, the salty snack she would pine for as a kid. Thick soft butter spread on small cream crackers, salty black vegemite spread on top. She insisted on even numbers of crackers so she could sandwich two together, pressing them so hard that worms of buttery vegemite would ooze out of the cracker's holes to be licked off.

Alice's head looks like vegemite worms: yellow mixed with black and a few that were muddy brown, curls of butter turning greasy in the sun.

'It's like someone pressed your head too hard.'

'Is that supposed to be a joke?'

'Is your hair?'

Alice's eyes blink rapidly and her chest heaves. Her cleavage and face come up with splotchy red marks as if she is allergic to her emotions.

'How can you be so hurtful?'

January speaks slowly, thinking about each word this time, 'I just meant that …'

'Forget it.'

Alice rips apart the picture that she had shown her hairdresser on Saturday. She knew she could never be as thin or beautiful as the model in the photo, but at least she could have her hair. Her stylist said that it was *bang on trend* and that she looked *fabulous*, and for two days she had believed him; her curls looked exactly like the ones crowning the model's head: dark chocolate browns merging with lighter caramels twisting again into deep espresso. She had felt good, sexy; hell, even the Ana twins had given her a compliment this morning, and it wasn't even back-handed. Alice is angry at herself for even caring what January thinks; her self-esteem cannot be reliant on the whims of others. She is, after all, her own woman. Alice carefully lines up the strips of the torn picture and tapes it back together. She should give January a piece of her mind, but January will probably just take it without acknowledgement, like she does with everything that Alice gives her.

The silence between them is an awkward wall too high for January to scale. It is strange the things you miss when they are suddenly gone. January had never imagined a time when she'd grieve the loss of Alice's voice. Usually she lets the drone of vowels and the staccato of consonants wash over her, watching Alice's mouth forming unintelligible shapes. She has wondered if deaf people find talking ridiculous; if they see others' grimaces and twitches and think them barbaric. January misses the white noise of Alice's voice, quieting the tinnitus of her own thoughts.

January inches her head over their partition, ready to duck if Alice looks up. As usual, Alice's positive affirmation calendar taunts her –

Life is Precious, Make it Count.

January wonders what kind of fool needs to be reminded of that fact. Who on earth does not know that life is precious and is not paralysed by the thought? That each decision you make affects your life; that everything you do counts; that you may die tomorrow and what will your life have been? How can you live your life without the pressure to live up to it? The hot pink and orange of the words sear themselves into her retina; would ghost on her eyelids if she closed them. It is a wonder that something can be so upbeat, yet so threatening.

A little like Alice herself as she catches January's eye, and shoots her a look that makes January feel like one of those ducks at a fun fair. You can almost hear the ricochet of the BB as January folds back down to her desk.

Click. Crack. Ping.

January's hands shake as she tries to type, creating a free style of spelling not seen since the heady days before the invention of the dictionary. She'd drain her coffee to calm herself if she hadn't drunk it dry already.

January needs a break, a few minutes away from reality. She digs around in her bag to check that her book is safely hidden. It is a book within a book; the paperback romance *A Traitorous Heart* fits neatly into a carved hole in a hardback shell. She chose a classic: Hesiod, to act like lead to an x-ray, completely concealing the romance. It is a conceit so that people will think that she reads literature, instead of the bodice-rippers that thrill her.

'I need a cigarette,' January announces to no one in particular, but with a sideways glance at Alice.

Alice opens her mouth to deliver the usual speech but clips it shut when she remembers that she isn't talking to January.

Positive energy begets positive energy, Alice chides herself, repeating the mantra over and over again. When she looks up January has disappeared from view.

It is worse than January thought. Alice didn't even try to give her carcinogens speech; she didn't reach for her self-help book, mark January with the sign of the Red Cross, repeating 'Let the power of the patch compel you!'

No, January has her bag slung around her and is almost out the door by the time Alice looks up. Alice's eyebrows rise to her hairline and seem to drag her eyelids with them. Her mouth is an oval of surprise as January, head down searching through her bag, ploughs straight into A1. Winded and surprised, A1 grabs the straps of January's bag to steady herself, but she is already too far back on her stilettos and just succeeds in pulling them both to the ground.

As she lifts herself off the floor January half expects to find A1's frail body shattered underneath her.

'Why don't you look where you're going?'

A1 sits in the middle of the debris liberated from January's bag: old bus tickets, moisturiser, cigarettes and a lighter; an old lipstick rolls slowly underneath a desk and tampons are scattered like little white bullet casings from a spent Gatling gun.

'Oh my god,' A1 brays, 'I think it's broken.'

If it's a broken leg, she'll never race again, mate. The best we can do is put her out of her misery.

The gun is loaded and the safety is off ...

BANG!

'What are you doing, you freak?'

January realises her hand is cocked and puts on the safety before holstering it. She scrambles on the floor, dumping whatever she can in her bag as quickly as she can.

Alice rushes over. 'Jan! Jan! Are you all right?'

'Her? What about me? I was the one almost crushed.'

'It's a good thing that silicone bounces then,' January says, and despite herself Alice smiles. No matter how hard she tries to stay angry with January, she never succeeds for long. January always makes her laugh.

A1 stamps her 'broken' ankle and stalks off; halfway to reception she remembers her injury and lamely limps with the help of A2.

Alice rolls her eyes as she helps January collect her things. January is too slow to reach her book before Alice does. The book lies butterflied on the floor, and as Alice picks it up January's secret vice is revealed. A *Traitorous Heart* indeed.

Alice turns over the hardcover book and laughs.

'I thought you were so deep, reading classics. But you read romance Jan? Really?'

Et tu Alice?

There is nothing worse than the sound of female laughter, nothing. January snatches the book from Alice's hand. She needs to get away from this.

'Jan, wait. I didn't mean ...'

The door clips off the rest of Alice's sentence before it reaches January. She is already on the stairs, her breath struggling to keep up.

Four years ago, January discovered the only place she could hide from Alice was with the smokers. At the mere mention of the word 'cigarette' Alice crinkled her nose. January bought her first pack of smokes that day, becoming a closet non-smoker. A couple of months into her ruse a man – young, cute and on the fast track to cancer – asked if he could bum a ciggie. He'd pay her back when he got paid.

She passed over her weathered pack and he lit one.

'Geeze. That's stale. How long have you had that in your bag?'

'A couple months. I'm trying to give up.'

He smiled and nodded his head.

'I tried once too. Decided I liked it too much. Mind you if they tasted like this I just might. You should sell the idea. The stale ciggie plan. You'd make a mint.'

'Maybe.'

January thought that she could be alone with her thoughts on these mini-breaks from Alice. What she hadn't counted on was how damn sociable smokers are.

They smile in recognition as you stumble outside in the rain. They huddle in groups against the wind, lest it take their precious flame away.

They ask for a light.

They bum a ciggie.

It is the closest January has got to a group of friends. A friendship in miniature, where commitment is measured in the burn of tobacco racing along rice paper a couple of times a day. It is like they are war buddies; people who in a normal time would not have met or, for that matter, liked each other. But the battle has brought them together, made a family of the few that remain. January can hear

Taps in the wind as another comrade falls to the enemy, their arms patched and their mouth stained with gum.

Today, January needs a smoke. Her head pounds in the daylight. Today, she can understand why they come out here; the physical need to calm down, to breathe deeply again. It could be a form of yoga, but for the smoke. Today, January finally feels like she belongs.

Part of the reason January likes the smokers so much is that they have no regard for death. How can you when you willingly shorten life every day, with every heavy breath? Death for them is not a spectre. It is not something that creeps into their life and makes a home in their pores. They don't think about their own death like January does. The thought of their mortality doesn't paralyse them, tainting each decision with doubt. Every puff they take, they thumb their nose at death; each breath is the strongest affirmation of life January has ever known.

The smokers' garden: a hard bench open to the elements, usually packed with smokers side by side, sharing their body warmth with each other like survivors; a couple of sad trees clinging to life in a container, cigarette butts as a mulch despite an insistent sign on a container of sand – *SMOKERS PLEASE*.

January pulls out a pen and scrawls *THEMSELVES*, underneath.

She fishes around in her bag. The packet of cigarettes she bought a few months ago is unearthed, a little torn but OK. She fumbles with lighting the cigarette, having only ever held one. Her flame falls victim to the wind a couple of times before she remembers to cup her hands around it.

The first hit of smoke sears her lungs, shutting all her airways violently. She coughs as if trying to bring up a lung. January can see now why people do this; it's so relaxing. She learns to take small drags on the cigarette and mixes it with air, as if she is tasting a fine wine. A little easier, but still there is burning pain. She wonders what dedication you must need to become addicted to these things in the first place.

January closes her eyes so that she can concentrate on her breath; in and out, in and out … but all she can hear is their laughter and Alice, even Alice, laughing at her. Her frown pinches her already tight brow; she feels as if a migraine is coming on, as if embarrassment was not enough of a malady.

Smoking does nothing to calm her down; she is twitchy, her head hurts even more and she feels ill. The throb in her head keeps rhythm with her heaves as January vomits into the ash-pot. The sand soaks up the liquid, leaving the little food she has eaten today mixed with cigarette butts. It reminds January of that guy in high school who was so drunk he sculled a bottle of beer filled with ash and butts, and promptly puked. The image of him bent over spewing out foamy beer and ash turns her stomach, and she vomits again.

Pity the poor smoker who finds her there. Sneaking out for a quiet cigarette, only to become nurse to that strange girl who holds a cigarette but never lights it. She tries to help; tries to hold back her own retches as she pulls January to the bench.

January smiles at her, bile still staining the corner of her mouth. The fishy smell of it hangs heavily in the air; the woman has to breathe in through her mouth. Oh wind! Why have you abandoned us now?

She croaks: 'I ought to give up,' before she leans over and vomits again.

It is this kind soul who drags January back to the office, desperately hoping that every jerk won't set her off vomiting again, as the only receptacle to hand is her new purse; picked up in the weekend, the last payment made.

It is this kind soul who insists that January be taken to the emergency room; or at least to a doctor to be checked out, and who says it is obvious to her that January will need a few days off to recover.

It is this kind soul who, looking down at the pack of crumpled cigarettes in her hand, is reminded of the yellow bile mixing with ash and other cigarette debris, and thinks that she might just give it a miss today.

At the hospital, January feels a little embarrassed to have been at the mercy of others; to be so helpless that she could not do what was necessary for herself. She silently thanks the woman, and thanks the Universe that it wasn't Alice who found her. She would have lorded it over January for the rest of her days.

She shudders as the cold liquid from the drip hits her system. It feels like all the veins in her body have run dry, the walls collapsed together and stuck; the saline is a gentle rain in a drought, coaxing her sluggish blood to move. She absently pinches the skin on the back of her hand and marvels at how it becomes tighter and tighter as she is slowly filled with fluid. The same can't be said about her migraine. It is still pulsing in her temples when the drip is empty. The nurse gives her two pain relief options: paracetamol orally, or by suppository. January considers asking for a doctor who might give her something a little more glamorous, a little more rock 'n' roll than something you can buy at a supermarket; but then she'd have to wait, and she runs the risk of pissing off the nurse, who will be removing that drip needle at some stage. January opts for the oral despite the protests of her stomach, as she has suffered enough humiliation today and doesn't want to add the indignity of dropping trou to that list.

On the way home she regrets her decision, as the taxi lurches around another corner and the drugs dissolving in her empty stomach nauseate her. She pays the fare with a hand clamped firmly across her mouth and is barely out of the taxi before she vomits into the bush outside her front door. It is only water and the two white pills, a little blurred at the edges.

It takes all her concentration to grab some water from the kitchen and make it to her bedroom without spilling any. Each step she takes seems to take a million years. When she finally collapses into the soft bed it feels as though it engulfs and embraces her, and she sleeps the dreamless sleep of the exhausted.

two

January's phone buzzes beside her ear just loud enough not to be ignored. She opens one eye to look at it and the word *WORK* shouts at her. January stuffs the phone under her pillow until the vibrations die away, but before she can take a breath it begins again. This time it is *ALICE* calling. January throws the phone across her room, not caring if she breaks it, and for a moment the room is silent. It is long enough for January to close her eyes and try for oblivion again.

Until the land line rings.

January opens her eyes. She can trace her flatmate's footsteps from the kitchen to the lounge and down the hall to her door. He doesn't bother to knock; he pushes the door wide open.

'The phone's for you.' He slurps his cereal, spills some milk on the floor and rubs it in with his foot.

January puts her pillow over her head and wishes that she was still asleep.

Her flatmate is still at the door. 'You're going to be late.'

'I'm not going in.'

'Another sickie eh? Or is it a mental health day?'

'Leave me alone.'

'I'd be glad to. But that Alice chick is persistent. Called yesterday and the night before …'

'Fine,' January glares at him until he gets the message and slopes off to the kitchen.

She pulls on her old track pants and a sweatshirt over the t-shirt she's been sleeping in. Her feet are bare, and she steps in the puddle of milk left by her flatmate.

Bloody ... flatmate!

It is funny how she can't bring herself to curse him by name. Is it true that if you name something then you have power over it? She doesn't know, but it seems to her that to name something you have to give a little bit of yourself. He already uses her shampoo – isn't that enough?

She picks the phone up from the arm of the couch.

'Hello?' January's voice is scratchy and shaky, a performance that has taken many years to hone.

'January? It's Alice. I missed you yesterday. Are you coming in?'

'I'm still not well.'

The flatmate is at the lounge door with his jacket on. He wags his finger at January and then mimes his nose growing just like Pinocchio. His lopsided smile is a challenge which January answers with the finger. He picks up his bag and waves goodbye. January throws a cushion at him but is too late – the front door has already slammed behind him.

Alice prattles on. 'It's just ... Well, you know, if you take more time off you need a doctor's certificate.'

'Doesn't a trip to the emergency room count?'

'You know how HR are.'

January weighs up her options. A visit to the doctor is costly, both in time and money, and even though it is pay day she can think of more interesting things to spend forty bucks on.

'I'll see you soon, Alice.'

She digs through her wardrobe for something to wear. Everything seems too constricting after a couple of days in t-shirts and baggy pants. She's not ready for the outside world with its buttons and zippers; she's so comfortable and cosy at home. But what would she do at home for one more day? She's read all her books; the only thing left to do would be to watch the crap that passes for daytime TV: those touchy feely shows (but not in the interesting R18 way) that seem to be able to cure all a person's woes in their allotted half hour slot: *Book me in for my twenty-three minutes of psychiatry, I feel a realisation coming on.*

January dresses as if she is attending a funeral: black on black on black. Thick cotton tights and a form-fitting turtle neck, merino, which makes her skin tingle before the itch dissipates. Over these, a black woollen dress, nipped in at the bodice with a full skirt; the hem falls just above the knee. She skips the concealer under her eyes, hoping that the dark circles will give the impression that she is, in fact, too sick to be at work and that she will be sent home.

But no one says anything remotely helpful when she mopes into the office. The only comment from A1: a pathetic *You're late*, which is what she says every day anyway. No one says she looks like death warmed up and that she should have stayed at home and here's a taxi chit because you shouldn't be walking in your condition. No one even looks up when she walks to her cubicle except Alice.

'You look much better than you sounded on the phone, Jan.'

'I don't feel like it. I think I'm going to throw up.'

Alice moves her papers away from the cubicle wall she shares with January.

'Well, if you're not up to work ...'

'Please say you'll cover for me while I take a nap in the photocopier room.'

'Actually,' Alice leans over the wall and whispers, 'I thought you might like to help me with a special project.'

'What special project?'

'The social club Matariki party.'

'But that's a month away.'

'Three and a half weeks, and there's so much to do. Venue, catering, decorations …'

Alice unfolds her project plan – the spreadsheet stretches over three A4 pages that have been taped end to end. The tasks are printed in different colours, and each day and hour is accounted for. January wouldn't be surprised if this conversation was planned and mapped out on Alice's sheet, but Alice folds it away before January can confirm that.

'Thanks Alice. But I'd rather stick to data entry.'

'Aw, c'mon Jan, it'll be fun.'

'You know me Alice. I'm just not that … social.'

'Look, you can do the decorations. That's easy. Please.'

January thinks about arguing, but Alice will eventually wear her down anyway, like water dripping on a stone. If she accepts now at least she won't have to listen to Alice plead for the rest of the day.

'Fine.'

'Thanks Jan. Here's my brainstorm about the decorations, but y'know, whatever you do will be fine.'

Alice hands January a board covered with pictures from magazines, quotes from printers and a floor plan of the venue.

Searching the internet for Matariki decorations makes the minutes that slip by less excruciating than usual. January has managed to look busy all day without actually doing any work at all.

She decides to treat herself to a new book; at least a new-to-her book. The second-hand bookstore is in an underground arcade; its old book smell competes with the butter chicken from the food court a few metres away. Next door to the bookstore is a music shop, where you can learn your instrument of choice for a low, low price. Today someone is learning the trumpet; the parps punctuate the quiet of the books. Towards the back of the store, tucked between the adult erotica and the popular fiction, is the romance section, like a bridge between the genres.

January runs her fingers along their coloured spines, each one a visual synopsis. Pure romance is pink, historical purple, light blue if you feel medically inclined. January's hand stops at the red spines; so obvious, red the colour of lust, the colour of desire. She picks one at random, not bothering to read the blurb. She also picks up another book just in case someone asks what she bought.

The trumpet heralds her arrival at the counter, and the man smiles at her as he adds up the prices.

'You'll enjoy this one. I'm a bit of an ornithologist myself.'

'I'm sorry?'

He picks up the book – *New Zealand Native Birds – An Illustrated Guide*. 'Bird watching, eh? Where are you going?'

January shrugs, 'Botanical gardens.'

'Not much to see there. Except for ducks.'

'I like ducks.'

Wah wah wah, the trumpet says as January leaves the store and hops on the escalator. She shoves the books in her bag before she walks past her usual bookstore, where she buys magazines and other novels. January is sure that the clerks can see her shame plainly on her face. Her pace quickens before she can see them shake their heads in disgust and laugh at her behind their hands.

three

January dreams: sunscreen and cut grass tang the air. Twilight confuses colour, making the world look as if it has been shot by a Lomo camera, the colours soft and saturated. She dreams of strawberry pips and picnic rugs, the wool making her skin tingle through her thin dress – or is that because his hand brushes against her leg? Her smile is coquettish; over her shoulder with downcast eyes, her eyelashes skimming her cheeks. He tilts her chin up and crushes a kiss on her lips; he tastes of strawberries. They need to be alone, now. Everywhere they go there are people, people. Late summer still warms the skin and people stay out as late as they can, storing up heat to tide them through winter. Surrounded by light and people he pulls her hand and they run. Then it is dark and rough. His whiskers at her neck, his coat on her thigh, the tree she is up against rubbing the skin between her shoulder blades; is this what love is? All she can think about is the bird that sings under the street light not knowing that it is night. She sighs for it and for a moment her pity is visible as it is chilled in the air. He is gone and so is summer; the leaves are turning brown on the limbs that held her so firmly.

She wakes to find the remnants of skin under her nails. The heat of the blanket and the weeping wound on her leg have bound the sheet against her. Light has flooded her room, her allotted daily fifteen minutes of sunshine barely making it worth opening the curtains. As winter approaches the minutes will become less and less and the damp in the corners will make the whole room musty and cold. She strips her bed; this is not how she planned to spend her Saturday. She peeks out the window. At least it is sunny so she can get this lot dry. January stuffs her sheets into the washing machine and flicks it to hot wash. When her eczema is this bad she needs everything to be clean, clean. She is like a walking wound.

Had she known she would have bound her hands in the thick heavy socks she keeps in her beside cabinet, taping the tops to her wrists. Futile, but it buys a few hours as her sleeping form fights against the tape.

Had she known she would have taken more vitamins, found new creams, and worn pure cotton.

She would have given up dairy, wheat, meat, air, anything.

But she did not know. Again and again through the night her fingernails had sought the spot, satisfying, until her flesh was reduced to a sodden mess, raw and weeping.

She watches as her blood swirls and gurgles down the shower's drain. The water bites at her knee, but the pain is good. It reminds her that she is alive. The white noise of the water clears her mind, giving her room to think. She looks at the wrinkled pads of her fingertips and shudders with disgust as she shuts off the shower.

The steam in the bathroom blurs her reflection in the mirror. A good thing too: her hair has been at once both tamed and made wild by the water; it wraps around her neck like seaweed on a sinker. She flips her head to the side, wrings out her hair and wraps it in a towel.

The bathroom cabinet is a graveyard of misplaced hope. January runs her fingers along the row of jars, each of their promises broken on her skin. Still she looks for a miracle, the cream that her skin won't react to; of course, the world being as it is, the more expensive the cream, the better. This one, a pretty little jar, made her eyes swell up despite the gold lid and the cream that smelled a little like roses. It is one way to get rid of wrinkles; her crows' feet had smoothed out over puffy watery eyelids.

Nothing here will help her skin, but still she persists. January wipes the mirror and suddenly her face comes into focus. Against the white of the towels her eyes look greener; less like a murky pond and more like the sea. She daubs cream around her eyes with the ring finger of her left hand in the way all the magazines have told her is correct.

With her towel wrapped firmly around her, January dashes from the bathroom to her bedroom. She opens her wardrobe and is stumped. Sartorial decisions cannot be rushed, particularly before her first cup of tea. As a stop gap January pulls on her sweatshirt and track pants; their texture odd against her naked skin.

January tip-toes around the flat. Is he even home? The question leaves her flat-footed. Most Friday nights he spends with his girlfriend, but even when he is not here he is; January can see evidence of him all over the house. A shirt he peeled off and left on the floor, his shoes kicked off in the hallway. She can even smell him as she walks into the flat; his odour leeches out of his room and through the flat. Sometimes, the voice of David Attenborough invades her mind:

Here, his movements can be traced by the trail he leaves behind: a dirty glass here, a newspaper there. A full-grown male can easily destroy a nest within a few minutes of entering.

If she could, January would happily live alone. Then she could indulge her desire to have matching cutlery, a nice couch and matching ottoman, a gorgeous rug on hardwood floors. She has looked at small one-bedroomed flats, studios and bedsits. Almost anything she can afford is damp and cramped, devoid of sunlight. She would be stretching herself to live like that with power and a phone line on top.

There would be no money left to buy her couch or rug. So for now she has to share her space with anyone she can put up with.

January fills the kettle and turns it on. As she waits for her tea to brew, she attempts to scrape off dried egg from her white dishes, but just like her flatmate it stubbornly clings on. Buying these was her first step towards leaving her student lifestyle behind. She was so happy that day to have something so pristine, new, without chips and the hairline cracks that start to go black as you use them. Her kitchen, in her mind, would be as pristine as those plates; it would be a place worthy of housing them. Unfortunately, her flatmate has taken advantage of this resolution, leaving his dishes for January to wash. She has thought about just leaving them, about slipping back into that comfortable way of life again, but she can't. Dishes must be washed every night, not left to pile up, unloved.

Dinner plates, side plates and bowls sit in neat stacks of six in the cupboard. Any day now she's expecting him to break a side plate, and the set will be ruined. She knew she shouldn't have bought this set. Not yet. But the deal was too good to pass up. January would leave the cupboard door open to admire them if she wasn't so clumsy. It would be just like her to clip the door and black her eye.

She considers hiding the plates in her bedroom, but then they'd have nothing to eat off, since she has thrown their op shop mismatched plates away. She has filled her room with the things she will have in her own home: a small love seat heaped with cushions, framed prints to hang on her walls, lamps for mood lighting. If there was an earthquake she would be lost under her books and cushions, her nick-nacks and dreams. As if her dreams do not already crush her.

January hugs her tea to her chest as she presses her ear harder against his door. There is no snoring from his room; perhaps he did stay away last night. It must be a luxury to wake up beside your lover. He has taken to calling her his partner, another annoying habit January would be happy to live without. But it would be nice, to be somebody's partner.

Partner.

January laughs as she imagines herself dusty and trail-worn. She ties the reins to a post and tips her hat.

Pardner.

Great. Next time he says it she'll giggle under her breath imagining chaps and spurs, as if the tweeness of the word isn't comedy enough.

The washing machine chugs into a spin cycle and January waits for the knock of protest on the wall. Nothing. As she suspected, he must be with his girlfriend.

Today, now that May has finally given up its battle with winter and is retreating, she covers every inch of her body in black: top, trousers, socks, even fingerless gloves to protect against the chill. She slips on her new boots, cowboy in style and ankle in length. January had maxed out her credit card to get them but she couldn't wait to pay them off; it would have taken at least three paydays. The heel is a little shorter than she would normally wear, but it is Saturday and she is trying to look casual – even though she has agonised for the past half hour about this particular outfit.

She dries her hair but the length of it and its curl seem to absorb the moisture in the air. The water that is forced out by her hairdryer seems to settle back as her hair cools down. The potions that she usually uses to coax it flat will just irritate her skin, so January gives up and pulls a beret over her head. The long strands of hair left out will eventually dry into ringlets and she will look cute enough, provided that her hat stays on her crown.

January checks in her bag for her book. It nestles between the pages of the hardback in the hope that great literature will pass into the romance as if by osmosis. Even though Alice now knows the truth, January will not give up this facade. There are more important people than Alice to impress. It jostles with the bird-watching book, a notebook and a pair of binoculars as she slings the bag around her. She struggles with the front door, her hands full with a picnic rug. She drapes it over her bag and hopes she doesn't trip on it up the stairs.

The houses in her neighbourhood are huge. Some, a long time ago, were split into flats and others have been renovated, reclaimed by modern families too small to fill their rooms. The street is lined with trees that were probably planted when these houses were built. In the summer they sizzle with cicadas, but they are silent now except for the groaning of limbs straining against the wind.

As she rounds the corner her heart pounds, as if she was meeting an old lover.

The yellow house on the hill below is visible as soon as she steps on the viaduct. Black tiles on the roof. A round room; no, it is a turret. Someone brave painted this house; someone so proud of their home that they wanted the world to see it, gold against the grey green of foliage. Is this how prospectors feel when the glint of gold shines out from the sludge? Do their hearts pound with the same excitement?

'My house.'

If only.

If it was hers, the turret would be a library filled with books she has read. At parties people would marvel at how well read she is. Gracious, January would laugh it off: *In a space like this who couldn't lose themselves in a novel?*

Then they would gaze out the windows, tall and narrow, curving around almost 270 degrees. Window seats, yes! Window seats piled high with cushions, made from old kilim rugs. They would sit at the window seats and stare out the window at the houses that climb up the hills and the angry grey sky; the perfect place to curl up and read. January would be generous with her books, even though they would be hardcover and leather-bound, instead of jealous and possessive like she is with her paperbacks. They would ask to borrow them and she would say: *I never lend anything that I can't give away.*

And she would hand over the books with a smile. Not caring if they will be returned. Nor if the bindings will be broken, the pages dog eared and passages underlined. In fact January's collection of books would sport notes in the margins, written in a tidy hand with an HB pencil. Witty and provocative thoughts of January herself, of course.

But not just her thoughts: her conversation would be clever as well. In her house the banter would be easy and friendly; her guests would laugh at the jokes she made – on purpose, not stomach-churning laughter at a phrase said out of turn and mistaken for something else. Here in this world, he would slide his hand around her waist so that everyone would know that they belong together.

But January knows that in this world, the real world, they don't, and as she turns the corner, the house and the fantasy are suddenly out of view.

The main gates of the Botanical Garden are at the other end of the street. January slips into the garden in the gap between the houses and the fence line. At this end, the fence is no longer wrought iron and brick, but wooden picket that is grey-green with exposure and age. January walks further into the gardens to her favourite tree, what she thinks of as *her* tree, an old oak that grows prone to the ground towards the street as if it is trying to escape, and in some way it has succeeded: the fence has been cut away underneath one of its great branches. It is the favourite of many – there is a plaque at its base that bears a poem written for it, and when the weather is warm, January must arrive early to secure her spot. But now the world is turning to winter she is alone with her tree. She spreads the rug out beside it and wishes she had brought a cushion as she leans against the trunk.

She had discovered the tree on her first visit to the gardens, and sitting on its trunk, so like a park bench, she saw the yellow house for the first time too. She has loved that house for many years, long before she knew that he lived in it.

She is close to the house here: only across the road and up fifty or so steps, but far away enough that they won't notice her. If anyone did notice, she would say that the binoculars were for bird-watching; that she is … what did that man say? An ornithologist. But no one has ever noticed January.

She can see their reality cradled in the arms of her tree; the branches of the old oak broach the void between her world and theirs. She watches them through the criss-crossing branches like they are wild animals at the zoo. Or perhaps they cage her, the interloper, keeping her at a safe distance.

She cracks her book open and it reveals itself like a virgin under the expert fingers of a deft lover. Immediately January becomes engrossed in the book: so engrossed she hardly notices the changes around her. The rest of the city falls away; she is alone in an ancient forest. Her hair wins its fight with humidity and gravity; her unruly curls become lustrous waves that fall tamely down her back. Her cheekbones rise, stretching her green eyes into the perfect almond shape, veiled with heavy black lashes. Her limbs lengthen and her waist narrows; her hips gently flare out. Her breasts swell against the flimsy material that barely protects her modesty.

The forest is silent, meaning only one thing: a predator is nearby.

January bites her full lips, moistening their ripe redness. Her breathing becomes rapid as her heart beats faster; her blood flushes her creamy skin. Every sense is heightened, and despite the terror, January feels something else. The excitement arouses the core of her womanhood. She should run; she should protect herself like all the other creatures in the forest, but the allure of the predator has her rooted to this spot. Something inside her wants to face the ravenous beast. It is as if she recognises her own hunger.

From her tree she spots him first, as naked as she; the pelt around his waist unable to disguise his excitement. He pauses and closes his eyes, searching for her scent. She gasps as his body, so fluid in motion, becomes like stone; his muscles taut in readiness for the hunt. The wolves around him have already picked up her scent; they pant and growl in anticipation. They are silenced by his look. It is as if he is communicating with them with his mind; as if he is one with them. He is pure alpha-male. She lets her eyes feast on his glistening chest, the ripple of his stomach, and the power of his thighs. She gasps as she looks up again. His eyes lock with hers and she is powerless. The pack surrounds her and she cannot escape him; she is his for the taking. He advances and she holds her ground. She would happily give her throat to him, to die in exquisite pleasure as he bites deep into her flesh ...

Despite the dark, January can sense him. She closes her eyes to catch the smell of him. His coat smells musky and mildewy at the same time, like the smell of scrim. Like the smell of sex. January is too caught up in her senses to realise that he has already found her. He pushes her against the tree and crushes a kiss out of her. This is how it always is for them: stolen moments in the dark shadows. When she finally breaks free, the steam that rises from her lips seems to be his breath not hers, as if he has taken hers away. January suddenly feels weightless. She hugs him a little too tightly, the guilt of their lust making her feel unsteady, like she needs something to anchor her to the ground. He always feels as though he is stable, an old Victorian building with well-grounded foundations. He pushes her further up against the tree, pulling her thighs against his hips. She cannot help herself: the scratch of his coat makes her sensitive skin itch, but it just stimulates her even more. Occasionally, if January allows herself to think, sex with him is like being an extension of his hand, and she feels sickened by it. Her mind wanders and she thinks about her, the wife, and what it would be like to make love with this man somewhere private and with candles, and then her body takes over again, loving the weight of his body against hers and the urgency of his need.

There is no need to think. Just feel.

She loves the feel and smell of his coat. He never seems to take it off, and it has moulded to the contours of his back and shoulders. The rough texture of the wool reminds her of running her hands against the peeling paint of the weatherboards at her childhood home; it is comforting despite the rash the wool brings up on her cheek. She bites his shoulder, his coat muffling her cries as his pounding subsides.

January has no idea how long she has slept. Without the light from the houses the street lamp throws odd shadows and January joins them, another black stripe across the orange-tinged street.

Tyger, Tyger ...

This has to stop. It was crazy enough in summer, but now she could die of exposure: the heat has gone from the earth and taken her cover of leaves with it. Her bower has been destroyed. How romantic would it be for him to find her still and blue-lipped in the morning? No, it is time to stop.

A starling is singing to a street light, confusing it for the sun. January wonders if it has any relief or if it sings perpetually night and day. Poor deluded thing. She is not sure why she feels so sad for it but its song is suddenly unbearable. She can't stay. She walks home, alone again.

The door of her flat creaks, the wood swollen with the damp of the night. She tries to sneak, but the hallway is littered with booby traps. Her toe is stubbed against steel-capped work boots, a jacket crumpled on the floor threatens to trip her and socks placed inexplicably on a shelf frighten the breath out of her. It is a wonder that she makes it to her room alive.

Alone in her bed, January's mind wanders back to a room filled with candle light and flowers, a room where they could take their time, where he doesn't have to hurry home to someone else.

She chides herself as she examines the scrapes on the palms of her hands where she steadied herself on the tree, each scratch and bruise a reminder: *This is not fantasy. This is real.*

She sleeps soundly, at least one itch satisfied.

four

The longest night of the year sure is living up to its reputation. the social club's attempt at warding off S.A.D. is just … sad. Matariki is a tease. They're celebrating that it is all downhill to summer, but truthfully winter still stretches ahead for another two months – maybe longer, given what passes for spring in this city.

What a perfect end to the day I've had. January's gulp of icy lemonade threatens to set off a migraine as she feels the cold leech down into her jaw and tighten the muscles in her face.

Sip. Sip. January swipes a straw from behind the bar and looks around.

Bloody Thursday night office parties. The reason why they are always scheduled on Thursday is threefold. 1 – Punters are unlikely to get themselves terribly drunk if they have to work the next day. 2 – It is easier to get a private function room during the week than the weekend. Finally, 3 – who wants to spend Friday night with the geeks from the office?

January has flaked on the decorations. She'd forgotten she agreed to organise them until Alice had asked about them earlier in the week: too late to get anything professionally printed: banner or balloons.

H-A-P-P-Y-M-A-T-A-R-I-K-I. Each letter stretches the span of an A4 sheet and is tacked on the wall, as permanent as the sentiment behind it. With a few clusters of balloons, the room has been transformed … into a room with a few balloons and a hastily printed banner.

At first glance the groups of people seem as randomly placed as the balloons, but the packs and pecking order established in the office stay true outside of it. A murder of managers, black suits and constricting ties, frown into their wine, a flock of geeks try to out-lame each other with their ironic t-shirts and their micro-brewery beer, and a pride of those who have lost all of theirs attempts to dance in the corner.

The piles of food are untouched. A1 examines each piece of food, the smoke rising from her ears as she calculates how many calories there'd be in every bite. Perhaps if just one pastry passed over her lips she would begin to swell up uncontrollably, her body so starved that it started to convert the air around her into fat. January narrows her eyes to send tempting pastry thoughts towards the buffet but alas, A1 must have been a Girl Guide at some time in her life: she has come prepared with an emergency baggie of celery sticks.

Mmmm. Celery.

Then January remembers the best way to serve tomatoes – juiced, vodka-ed, a dash of Tabasco and celery to garnish.

Mmmm, celery.

January elbows her way to the bar. 'Bloody Mary.'

'Sorry love,' the barman looks at her drinks voucher. 'These are only good for house wines and tap beers.'

'I'll get it for you, January.'

Great, she's ended up next to Ted, her manager. From the flush in his cheeks it would appear that he's burned through his three free drinks already.

'A Bloody Mary for you and a red for me. Cheers.'

'Cheers.'

'Great party, eh? Alice has really outdone herself.'

'Apart from the decorations.'

'Yeah, well .. ' Ted lifts up his glass. 'I guess we're drinking what she saved in decorations.'

'I did the decorations, Ted.'

'Oh. Ah ...'

A surge of people come to the bar and Ted is pushed forward. His hand lands on January's shoulder.

'Careful, Ted. You've already bought me a drink, people will start to talk. And sexual harassment is such nasty business.'

Ted's face reddens and he backs away from January. 'Well, must circulate ...'

January lift her glass. 'Cheers.'

January leans against the bar, counting off the minutes with each sip on her straw. She'll drink her free drinks and then she'll go home; hopefully the alcohol will blot out the wasted hours here.

Alice looks as if she is having the time of her life. For some reason she invited a date along. The guy doesn't look like a gormless freak, but if he's laughing at her jokes he may just be mentally defective.

Alice moves her hand on top of his. January suddenly feels like a voyeur. The gnawing in her organs doesn't abate with a sip of her drink, and not for the first time tonight January wishes that it were something stronger. Cyanide perhaps.

It is the first awkward moment of a romance – when you lie about little things, like your love of blue cheese, just to appease the other. Then later you find that you both detest the stuff; that you were both being polite, and you fall into each other's arms laughing. The potential of intimacy is heady, and your entire being is focused on getting to know another. Each other's mind and moods are a mystery that you can't wait to solve.

January turns away, no longer able to watch; it is a reminder of what she cannot have. She sips her drink and then plays with her straw, stirring things up. It seems strange to her now, that just a few months ago she had no idea that he even existed. The man she tries not to think about all day. The man she turned mistress for. How often had she walked past him in the street not knowing, missed him as he walked into a shop? How did she not know of his existence? How could she not feel him around her, like a breeze goose-pimpling her skin? The enormity of that thought often makes her stop now, to marvel at the different faces of humanity on the street and wonder about their lives. Each of those different faces has a life that she is not privy to. What do they think of when they walk down the street? Where are they going? How can we all exist so close together, living in each other's pockets, and not know one another? The sea of faces that usually washes over her suddenly becomes concentrated and focused. She can see each person distinctly now; how a few millimetres' difference in the width of an eye, nose, mouth makes someone unique in the cookie-cutter sameness of our features.

It had been an ordinary day. The cobblestones made it almost impossible to keep balance in heels as she dodged people on the crowded street. The zip on her bag had refused to budge, overstuffed as it was with gym gear. The extra weight threw her off slightly so that, without intervention (divine or other), she'd continually be running in circles. As she ran across an intersection a sneaker shook itself free, and she didn't notice the loss until his hand gently landed on her shoulder.

'Excuse me. You dropped this.'

A Cinderella moment, spoiled perhaps by the ripe, sweaty sneaker he had in his hand rather than a beautiful slipper. But she silently thanked whatever god it was that it hadn't been her underwear instead.

'Thank you.'

'I think you need a bigger bag, Miss …?'

'January. Just January.'

His offered hand was smooth and strong; she wanted to place that hand upon her cheek.

'Well, January, you should look into a bigger bag. Or perhaps you should travel lightly.'

He turned and would have disappeared forever into the crowd had January not done the bravest thing in her life.

'Please, let me thank you properly. A drink?'

'If I wasn't married you'd be in trouble.'

With three words January began their affair.

'I like trouble.'

She's been teetering ever since. It was she who wanted no strings, no intimacy, no emotions. Yet it is she who now laments how their 'relationship' limps on but never gets anywhere.

January's straw gurgles in her empty glass. She looks up and sees that guy she thinks of as Limpy in front of her.

'Can I buy you a drink?'

'No thanks,' January waves him away with her drink vouchers. 'I'm fine.'

She sips a house red, the tannins staining her mouth a vinegary purple. She tries to catch Alice's eye, but to Alice there is no one else in the room. January wishes she knew how that felt. Alice will get to know her man more than January will or could ever know hers. Alice has more courage; she has opened herself to another human being in a way that January can't even imagine.

An interesting fact about celery. Being mostly fibre and water it uses more calories to eat celery than it provides to your body, so it's like eating nothing at all.

Another interesting fact about celery: it doesn't soak up alcohol they way a nice vol-au-vent would. January wonders if this was part of Alice's plan – buy pastry and get your entertainment for free – A1 does a good floor show. January wants to ask Alice, but she's busy fussing about the party – arranging food and talking to the bar staff.

'Do you want to dance?' Limpy, god bless, is a persistent pest.

January throws back her drink and her voice is strangled with the acidity of the wine. 'I need a refill.'

She orders another drink and sits on a bar stool just far away enough from the dance floor that she won't be dragged onto it.

A1 is aping on the dance floor with the rest of the office. They whoop and screech along with the music. A1 fixes her predatory glare on a hapless victim and reels him in with a curl of her sparkly pout.

Be careful mate! She hasn't eaten in years.

It is, bar none, the most disgusting kiss in the history of mankind. Tongues and saliva: it is carnage you just can't turn away from; an accident where you feel sorry for the victims and thank heaven you weren't involved.

An Ana unhinges her jaw and swallows her victim head first. A specimen of this size could quite easily ingest a man twice her weight. Thus satisfied, the creature will not need to feed for another decade...

A voice, which January is not one hundred percent sure is in her own head, pipes up: 'It's just a kiss. She doesn't mean anything by it. She's just drunk.'

January looks around for the stray voice. The only person it could have come from is A2, which seems impossible as her normal mouth piece's tongue is obviously occupied.

'It's a party; there will always be a few regrets in the morning.'

'Did you say something ...'

'Vanessa.'

'Sorry?' January says, like she has been caught with her headphones in.

'My name, January, is Vanessa. You've never bothered to ask.'

Of course she hadn't. January has always seen the twins as a single entity, incapable of living apart.

A1, finished with her prey, fixes her gaze on January and Vanessa. Territorial, she slithers her way across the dance floor and seizes Vanessa's hand.

'C'mon Nessa, come dance with me.'

A1 drags her shadow off again, and Vanessa reverts back to type. January pretends to get into the terrible music playing, bopping her head along. She pretends to understand the ritualised mating behaviour that surrounds her – the preening and promenading; the baring of teeth and flesh that is more aggressive than alluring; the touch of a misplaced hand.

She gulps down her drink and orders another, emptying her glass in almost one swig.

Her eyes close involuntarily as she remembers her own delicious union with him, his hands following the curves of her body. The itch of his coat against her bare skin made January scratch herself. The tearing of her flesh only heightened her arousal: she was suddenly aware of the textures on her skin. The rough bark under her palms, the soft material of her dress pushed up over her hips, the smooth wetness of his lips against hers and the sharpness of whisker inching through his skin which left anywhere he kissed red and itchy.

Whenever she sees his coat she longs to rub her cheek against it to recapture that moment. She bites her lips to get the feeling back into her mouth.

Her head is reeling with pheromones.

'Another red.'

'Are you sure love? I think you've had enough.'

'I'm not your love, and I have a voucher left, see?' January waves an old eftpos receipt in the barman's face. 'Wait. It's here. Just give me a second …' January digs around in her bag.

'How about I call you a taxi?'

'You can call me what you like, just not love.' January laughs at her joke but the barman is stony faced – he's heard it all before.

'OK, fine. I'm going,' January walks out of the bar. 'I'm gone.'

Outside the cold air sharpens her vision and her thoughts. January pulls her coat around her even though the alcohol has dulled her skin against the cold. A1 is out here; she has pressed her victim against the wall. They too are oblivious to the cold; neither has a coat on and in a few minutes they will probably be even less clothed as well. A1's skirt is pushed up and January imagines her skin goose-pimpled by pleasure, not weather. If she closes her eyes she can imagine his hand on her breasts, her thighs. She can imagine that the groans and sighs are from her throat. Her pace picks up as she walks past them. She needs to be safe, cocooned at home away from the hope of sex.

five

January shoves the door to her flat open with her shoulder, expecting resistance from the junk on the other side, but the door swings free. She shuffles her feet forward in case she trips over rugby boots, a shirt or a newspaper. Nothing. The hall is clear apart from her bag dumped by the front door.

There is something not quite right here.

The first thing January notices is the smell. She hadn't realised how accustomed to a smell you get until it is gone. How anyone gets accustomed to the musty smell of feet and unwashed sheets is a scientific miracle: perhaps an evolutionary safeguard to ensure women will stick with their partners through toe jam and dirty underwear. The fresh smell of lavender is not bad, quite pleasant in fact; but not *right*, not home.

Then there are the dishes. Not under a cushion in the lounge, but where she left them: clean and stacked in the cupboard. She counts the stacks again and again: each one is present.

It should have been obvious from the start. It is not the first time this has happened to her, but usually it is a little bit more dramatic: an acrimonious letter, a slammed door. Usually when flatmates leave in a hurry, they leave the place messy; they don't bother to clean up. If only she could afford to live here by herself, but she knows she will have to look for another cretin to share her space soon. Finding flatmates in winter is notoriously difficult in this city.

January wonders what horrors will welcome her as she opens the bedroom door. It could be the standard fare: used condoms in the corner, a collection of dust. There had been the writer who used the walls as his personal notebook, penning angsty poems about young love: the rhyme 'sexy' with 'complex-y' was a particular favourite. It had been a joy to January to paint over his 'art' with the buttery yellow paint that is standard in flats: the cheap paint that feels like chalk when it dries.

She opens the door and flicks on the light, preparing herself for the mess. What can the human eye see in a split second? What she sees is his bed, and then the linen on his bed, then his foot on the linen, his legs, his back and her naked buttocks pressed against his hips …

David Attenborough is in her head again:

The display of the rump indicates that the female is ready to mate. The male thrusts his penis into his obliging partner, rocking her violently so that her cervix will open in orgasm. The mating ritual can last anywhere between a few seconds …

The slamming door cuts January's gasp in two.

She realises that it is worse than she had thought: he has not moved out but moved his girlfriend in.

God, I'm living with a couple again.

The moronic cutesy talk, as each partner seemingly loses their wits as soon as the other is within the same room.

I wuv you!

I wuv you more!

The bathroom will be occupied for hours as they conserve water by showering together.

The fridge will become a booby trap of sex food. For what other purpose was whipped cream in a can created?

The bedroom door opens again. Her flatmate, sticky with sweat, his modesty (too late now) hastily covered by a towel.

'We need to talk.'

'I'm going out.'

January's bag, determined to stay and gawp, catches on the doorknob. The girlfriend appears in one of his shirts, her fingertips barely peeking out of his cuffs. She looks as if she is shrinking under the influence of him; that one day she'll wake up and realise that she is just an appendage of his.

'Is she all right?'

January is out the door before she hears his answer.

She has no idea where she is going; she just needs a hideout for a couple of hours. If she had bothered to learn the code for the alarm at the office she could hide out there, but who could have foreseen a time when she'd ever need to be there after hours?

She could go back to the party and join the sad few who are left. She could help Alice clean up and maybe stay at her flat. Although the way things were going when she left, Alice probably already has a guest tonight ...

She shudders and pulls her coat closer around her neck. Perhaps the wind will blow away the cloud cover and she could sleep under the stars? It is too cold, even if she's lucky and it doesn't rain. If she was still drunk she wouldn't care, but the horror at the flat has sobered her up pretty quickly.

Another drink is needed, at least to dull the memory. At this time of night the bars are just warming up – the bands that were supposed to start two hours ago are taking to the stage, half their rider in their stomachs already. She walks into the first bar she comes across. The drummer counts off the beat, making every move January makes seem mechanical. The singer new-new romantic; more rouged and mascara-ed then January has ever been in her life, slurs into the microphone. He can't help it really; it would be impossible to form words with that thing practically down his throat. It is a scene too intimate for January to watch any longer, and she is grateful for the lack of a mirror behind the bar.

She orders a hot toddy to at least get the feeling back in her fingers. The warm glass makes them prickle, like the icicles within are breaking free. January puts her glass down when she imagines the splinters racing in her bloodstream toward her heart, piercing and freezing it forever.

But it must have already frozen: she cannot see any beauty in the desperate pairing she sees around her. She watches two women share a hurried shot of confidence, their glasses barely touching the bar before they drag themselves on the dance floor, shaking their rumps like ovulating baboons. The drink does nothing to take the bitterness out of her mouth and so she leaves it half-empty on the bar.

Nowhere in the city is safe from this need to couple. Even the ordered supermarket with its truthfully harsh lighting is a hunting ground for the city's hopeless. January gave up on buying bananas years ago, when she realised how the way she placed her bunch in her basket would be interpreted by the other primates. At least in this light she can see their intentions clearly. A man winks at her over the broccoli. She wonders what fruit could be interpreted as *leave me alone*, but decides on an unequivocal scowl.

January wanders up and down the aisles, her basket as empty as the eyes of the check-out girls. She wonders what they've all done wrong to end up in this purgatory. But at least they have a purpose; they have a real reason to be here – it is not cowardice that keeps them from their home. She stares at a wall of tomato soup unable to make a decision because each can is essentially the same – water, tomatoes, sugar and seasoning. There are too many choices. What if the soup she chooses is too sweet, or too salty?

The notice board is just as crowded with decisions – does she want to learn drums or the secret of breath? Is she vegan-friendly, are pets OK with her? January rips a couple of numbers off the notices and shoves them in her pocket, where they'll slowly turn into confetti each time she shoves her hand in. Even if she doesn't call them, at least she has done something. She is sick of this semi-adulthood. She has been out in the world for many years now; shouldn't she be able to afford a place of her own by now? She rips another number off and detects another colour, another texture behind it. She crumples up the notice, its corners still stapled to the board. Hidden underneath is a small card, about half the size of a postcard, its edges scalloped and lightly gilded. Something about the size and the subject of the card make her mind connect it to the Tarot. It is as if the card hums with the promise of her future, holding secrets just waiting to be interpreted. She laughs the thought off, but somehow the imprint of it makes her want the card, and she pulls it free from the board.

It is a simple scene of time past: children dancing around a maypole. In a small typeface is the caption 'May Day', almost the only words on the entire card, save for a few handwritten words on the back:

Tell me a secret.

Reply in handwriting to ...

The message and a post office box, nothing else.

Normally something like this would creep her out: the image of cherub-faced children gambolling around a maypole, their over-large heads and eyes hinting at something more sinister Yet there is something engaging about the children as they weave around the pole, seemingly alive with colour. Their cheeks would have been described as ruddy in days past; now their parents would be worried about UV damage and smother them in sunscreen and hats. They play in a time that January is not sure ever existed. She has an almost medieval view about children: she swears that they are merely demons in disguise and that they cast a glamour over you so that you will do their bidding. People say that you feel differently when it is your own child, but to January that just strengthens her point. Witchcraft.

She is bewitched, and as soon as the word is thought the theme music from the TV show plays in her head – a soundtrack to her thievery. Although can it really be theft to take what is freely given? Is there really any ownership in a public notice board? Besides, if whoever put it there wanted more than one reply they would have made one of those tear-off posters. Instead they posted this small card that fits so well in the palm of January's hand.

She turns around and looks at the check-out girls. One, glazed-eyed and chewing gum, reminds January of a goldfish gasping for breath. It is the pop of her jaw as she chews and the faint orange glow of fake tan. None of them would care if she took the card; none of them would even notice. To be on the safe side, January pretends to search for her phone as she drops the card into her bag; she pulls the phone out and checks the time in the exaggerated manner of pantomime dames and high school productions.

The girl at the counter is unmoved by the performance, and continues to mark off the seconds of her life with a pop.

Pop.

Pop.

The gape of the girl's mouth must remind the lizard part of January's brain of yawning, because she feels as if she is running out of air. She heads for the taxi courtesy phone and grabs the receiver as if it is a life line to the outside world, comforted by the purr of the dial tone. No need to dial: someone is always waiting.

In the privacy of the taxi, January looks at the card again.

Tell me a secret ...

She wonders how she could ever narrow it down to one.

six

Adrenaline makes January walk faster. The wind whips around her and it seems as if her feet never touch the ground. She cannot help but smile, despite being on her way back to work. The beads in her fist, crushed tightly together, will leave small round bruises on her palm; the earrings' hooks dig in and scratch. Such is the impression of her first criminal act.

It was not a store that January would usually go into. The shop had reminded January of an old-fashioned sweet shop. The temptation of baubles and jewels had sparkled in large glass jars, like humbugs and acid drops. The women in the store had eyed them hungrily, like over-sized brats aching to spend their pocket money. The attentiveness of the shop assistants scares her: January always gets the feeling that they are either judging her or waiting for her to lift something, which she would never dream of doing. Until today. There is something perversely satisfying about shoplifting. It is like revenge for the raised eyebrows of the shop assistants, their fake cleaning around you, they way they make you feel as if you are a criminal when you take off your coat and lay it over your bag. Like you have something to hide. Today January reasoned if they were going to think the worst of her why not live up to that expectation? She was surprised at their lack of reaction; she had expected a chase down the street. Perhaps they are paid so little that they don't care:

not enough to chase someone down the street. More likely is that they didn't even notice, their attention drawn by someone else.

Olivia, O Olivia with your bright obsidian hair. Today you were an accessory to robbery and you don't even know it. The shop assistants were drawn to her, and January was left to her own devices in the store. January was the moon eclipsed by a far greater heavenly body. Olivia seems to radiate light; she is summer personified: all tanned skin and sandalled feet despite the winter chill in the air. Olivia the great, impervious to all that plagues men; a goddess on earth.

Of course he loves Olivia. January herself seems to love her. Although it is a terrible gnawing accusing love:

Why can't my skin be as clear?
Why can't my hair be as straight?
Why can't my stomach be as flat?
Why does he need me at all?

Why does he need January? Perhaps January gives him what no goddess would grant, but a mere mortal is happy to give away.

My dignity.

No, January chose this; she is in control. But somehow she still feels as if she has been duped out of something. Can you really make a choice if you have no options?

January felt compelled to follow Olivia when she saw her. Olivia's enticing scent drew January after her, with another pang of jealousy as she thought how lucky Olivia was to be able to spray on perfume without the searing heat of a rash newly formed. It was stupid, but January wanted a little recognition from Olivia; the smallest acknowledgement would have sufficed. The flare of a nostril, the narrowing of an iris; anything that would prove that January's relationship with him was not a fantasy; that she existed. Olivia's blithe indifference fed January's doubts.

It was a weird sensation. January at once wanted to be Olivia and destroy her. She imagined telling Olivia everything: shattering her perfect world just as a mirror shatters January's own illusions of beauty. Compared to Olivia, January feels like the before shot in a make-over show: untamed hair and problem skin. Her features aren't as fine, nor are her clothes. She longs to pull Olivia finally to earth, by telling her about the reality of the world. But the inherent danger in the plan stays her hand; Olivia would probably only feel pity for the girl who is nothing more than a glorified masturbation aid for her husband: as much pity as a person feels for ants trodden underfoot. Olivia's pity would be infinitely worse than not warranting recognition at all.

Olivia has everything January wants: beauty, a house and him. But now January has something Olivia wanted.

Olivia had been eyeing a particularly bright confection: a pair of earrings that cascaded from her lobes to brush her shoulders gently. Beads of red and amber clustered together like grapes so ripe they could have burst at any second, tucked in between small birds, there to sing the praises of Olivia, or perhaps to tell her secrets.

Like what your husband gets up to.

Against the blackness of Olivia's hair, the earrings transformed from the earthly to the ethereal. The lustre of the beads was like the intense beauty of a nebula: the birth of a galaxy. Olivia was the creator, the alpha and omega, and all would bend to her will.

It was at this moment that January knew she must have those earrings. At least to steal a little spark from Olivia's fire. It had been easier to steal from the gods than the myths would have you believe: all January had to do was wait until Olivia walked to the other side of the shop, with the assistants in her wake. The earrings had been replaced in their cradle; they swayed gently as if mimicking

Olivia's walk. January hesitated before picking them up. She held them to her lobes and admired the effect in the mirror. If she squinted she could almost believe she was Olivia; had she not the same dark hair and slim physique? The earrings lay on her palm, and she considered putting them back and walking away, but did not. She closed her fist around them as an assistant walked past, but she needn't have: the assistant didn't even acknowledge her. She waited a while, convinced that someone would notice, but nobody did, not even when she opened the door and the bell tried valiantly to nark on her. She even stood outside the store and watched Olivia, willing her to look outside before she finally turned and left.

Now they are hers. January can finally look at them in the safety of her cubicle. They are more beautiful than she had thought, perhaps more so now because they are a triumph. The afternoon is punctuated by the brightness of the beads, their colour brought out by the dull grey of her cubicle wall; brought out by the absence of anything else to distract the eye.

She wants to perform some sort of ritual to celebrate the first time she wears them, but when she finally gets them home temptation proves too much, and she roughly shoves them into herself like she is a teenage boy whose girlfriend has finally said yes.

The itching starts almost immediately. She has just enough time to admire herself in the mirror before the heat in her lobes overtakes the glow of the beads.

But she does not take them off, even when her lobes burn red; even when the skin on her neck raises itself into angry welts. She imagines them as fiery kisses: a rash formed by his stubbly cheeks. The pain makes her closer to him somehow.

Naked in her bed she imagines the sensation of his hands on her waist. Each nerve tingles as she feels his breath at her nape. Tonight he will be January's alone, even if he isn't there to share it. A fiction, whispered often enough, begins to taste like truth.

'I bought these for you, January.'

'But Olivia ...'

'Shh, I bought them so the world would know how I feel about you. Wear them always.'

'Always.'

January closes her eyes and she can feel his weight on her, his teeth tearing her neck and ears. The gentle sway of her earrings becomes more violent and the hooks begin to wear her skin thin; her lobes crack and weep. She bites her lip so she won't cry out, afraid that her voice will bring her back to reality.

Her earrings are still in as she drifts into sleep, dreaming of his whispers of love as her blood pools and scabs around the metal hooks.

She had ripped open the wounds on her ears as she removed them this morning. They had fused to her ears with dried plasma, as if they were becoming a part of her. She had taken comfort in that thought. Indeed since she has taken them out she still feels a faint throbbing, and wonders if this is what it feels like to lose a limb; if she closes her eyes she can still feel the beads swinging against her throat. She had tried to hide her eczema – wearing her hair down to cover it, the strands sticking to the raw skin and drying in hard clumps around her hairline. She had managed to sneak to her desk without a remark from Alice. The rash remains undetected as Alice leans over the cubicle wall and asks January if she'd like a coffee.

'Thanks Alice.'

She has finished going through her emails when she notices that Alice is not back. What is she doing? Probably gas-bagging in the break room, which means January's wounds will go undetected for a while longer yet.

When she gets back Alice looks as if she is about to burst, literally: her face is flushed, her eyes are wide and her chest heaves up and down. January tries to grab the coffee that Alice left to make ages ago – what was she doing? Growing the beans herself? – but Alice seems to have the mug in a death grip.

'I have news.'

January doesn't really have a choice; she won't be able to ignore Alice. If she doesn't engage in this, Alice will just go on and on. Best to get it over with and let her talk; hopefully she'll exhaust herself before the coffee gets cold.

'What news?' January reaches again for the coffee but Alice is too excited to notice.

'I was making our coffee … Oh yeah, here you go.'

January gulps her coffee. *A spoonful of caffeine makes the medicine go down …*

'… Anyway she said, and she should know, that Ted's leaving.'

'What?'

As if on cue Ted sticks his head out of his office door. January cheerily waves to him. His right eye twitches in recognition of her and he retreats back in.

'The stress is too much for him.'

January feels a small pang of guilt. Two years ago when Ted first started in his job, he was confident and determined to take the company forward. He tried team-building, introducing social events that he and Alice seemed to be the only ones interested in. He devised staff development programmes so the staff would be challenged and motivated to achieve. It's not like she meant to destroy his vision. It's just that January has an issue with corporate team-building. The idea of forcing people to interact with their workmates on their own time is repugnant to her. She feels that it is her duty to enlighten the powers that be that the workers are not interested in furthering the company: they just want their pay cheques. Don't they? No amount of touchy-feely-we're-all-in-this-together-mate will change that.

In two short years they have broken Ted into a neurotic, twitchy man. Half of his neurosis could be directly attributed to January herself. Her natural inclination to sarcasm and hypochondria seem to have irked Ted somewhat. Her last performance review had given Ted the twitch in his eye. It started out fine enough: Ted told January how well she was doing and January agreed. Ted suggested courses she could do to improve her performance.

'So if I do this course, I'll get paid more?'

'Well, not at once. But if it improves your performance then we can reassess the situation.'

'So I would be doing the course for nothing.'

'It would improve your performance and challenge you personally.'

'So basically, you get a more skilled worker at a chump's rate? I don't think so.'

Ted's eye had developed a lump; he rubbed it with his finger. It hurt to rub it, but it was a kind of delicious hurt that grounded him to the here and now. It was during times like these that Ted fantasised about taking a yacht around the Pacific, his skin turning leathery brown and his hair sun-kissed and highlighted. He was master of his world: things were done without question, orders were respected; in his little vessel he controlled all who boarded. He didn't control the sea, of course. A tsunami called January threatened to capsize his dream. He prodded his eye again and the Pacific sun was muted behind Venetian blinds.

'January. You don't have to do the course.'

'But if I don't do it then there's absolutely no chance of getting a raise, is there?'

'I didn't say that exactly.'

'But the only way I can get a raise is if my performance improves?'

'Yes.'

'And you think that my performance will improve if I take this course?'

'Well, yes.'

'So basically I have to take this course.'

'I guess so …'

'We'll see what the union say about that.'

Ted's eye had swollen. A sty was growing near his tear duct. He felt as if he had been punched in the eye.

'Fine. Shall we move on? Do you have any concerns, January?'

'Actually I do. I have found that whenever I walk into this building I begin to sneeze …'

Ted's eye began to water. He dabbed it with a clean tissue: each dab felt like a blow. His eyelids, swelling, were squeezing his vision out.

'So I think it may be sick building syndrome.'

'Like you thought we had Legionnaires'?'

'Better to be safe than sorry.'

'January. Are you sure you are suited to this job?'

'Careful, Ted. That sounds like constructive dismissal to me.'

Ted's eye had fused together now. He couldn't open it even with his fingers.

'Ted. There's something wrong with your eye.'

'Thank you, January.'

'No seriously …'

'Maybe we could finish another day?'

Ted had gone home with a blinding headache and a swollen eye. He took the next two days off and came back with an eye patch. It was not January's intention to start the pirate jokes; it just seemed obvious to her. Really, it was not her fault that they caught on. In a way Ted should have been happy; the whole office pulled together as a team, all of them dressed as seadogs, and a rousing 'Arrr!' greeted Ted each time he stepped out of the elevator.

Alice is still prattling on. 'That means his job will open up. Management.'

He's barely a corpse and already the vultures are circling.

'So are you going to apply, Jan?'

'I don't know.'

'It's a good opportunity.'

'You should apply, Alice.'

'You think I'd make ... January, your ears are bleeding.'

With the distraction of Ted, January foolishly thought that Alice wouldn't notice her scabby ears and the rash that encircled her neck like the evidence of a crazed lover's strangle hold.

'Does that mean someone is talking about me? I can't remember.'

'What happened?'

'It's nothing. Just a reaction.'

'A reaction to what?'

January tries to shrug off Alice's attention.

'It'll be fine in a couple of days.'

'How can you stand it? If I had a rash that bad I wouldn't come into work.'

'Well, if you insist. Here's that report I've been working on and I'll see you in a couple of days.'

'Seriously ...'

'I am serious. Look, I've got my coat.'

'Ted,' Alice calls into his office, 'We're going to lunch.' Alice doesn't give him time to answer as she and January sweep out the door. 'I'm taking you to my naturopath.'

This path seems unnatural to January: getting medical advice from some hippie quack. There must be something wrong with a place where you don't have to make an appointment to have your health assessed. The nagging consumer in her head tells her this man has a vested interest in selling whatever 'cure' he can, whether it is likely to cure her or not. Retail is retail after all, and sure, being talked into a hideous skirt by a pushy sales assistant is expensive and sucks, but it is nothing compared with being talked into something that could do irrevocable harm. Did this guy even go to med school, or just some hippie drop-out commune? She can guess what his diagnosis will be – too many refined foods blocking her chakras: the health of your liver will only cost you an arm and a leg. At least it's an extra half-hour out of the office.

Her fears are confirmed as she walks through the door of the place. The stomach-turning tang of vitamin B hangs in the air, reminding January of every hangover she has ever had. Row upon row of white plastic bottles give the place a pseudo-pharmacy feel, but these are filled with eye of newt and other 'cures' that have been in use for thousands of years so don't need rigorous scientific testing.

Dysentery and tapeworm! Proven cures for the modern plague of obesity! Used around the world for thousands of years to naturally control your waistline! Don't delay, talk to one of our lifestyle professionals today!

She expects a wannabe swami to float out, dressed in a fine white linen caftan and a turban, affecting a slight Indian accent to convince that he studied under the best in Mumbai. Alas, he is dressed in disappointing trousers and a polo shirt emblazoned with the franchise logo. He is annoyingly healthy looking and even more annoyingly happy. There is a slight orange tinge to his skin – fake tan or too many carrots? Whichever it is, it makes the icy blue of his eyes pop, just like your high school art teacher told you complementary colours would. January wonders if this is how he drums up business: by faking the intensity of his eyes, making it seem as if they could bore into your very soul, revealing the truth to him.

More disappointingly, his name is Robert. No Native American spirit guide name, no name reclaimed from lives past in Egypt, no ceremonial name passed from a long line of ancient Celt druids; not even an attempt to try and legitimise his practise by tacking 'Dr.' on the front. Just plain Robert, as emblazoned on his name tag: the kind you can get engraved at the key and shoe place for about five dollars while you wait.

'Alice. You are looking well, are you sticking to the plan?'

'To the letter. And it's working just like you said it would!'

'Alice, you know I can take no credit. I just showed you the path; you're doing all the hard work. I'm proud of you.'

January's innate scepticism is bitter in her mouth. She almost gags when she sees Alice giddy and blushing, falling over this man with gratitude.

'This is January.'

Robert pulls January's hair away from her neck, shakes his head and tuts like a mechanic. *Mate. It's not going to be cheap. Your alter-whose-anator is shot, and don't get me started on your condense-ma-cator.*

'I didn't want to come, but Alice insisted. It'll clear in a couple of days. I'm fine, really.'

'January, sometimes we think we're fine, but our bodies tell us otherwise. Is there anything troubling you?'

Apart from a six-foot carrot with legs? No.

Robert opens the door to his exam room and guides January in like the hostess on a game show showing off the prizes. *January! Come on down!* She looks back at Alice, who just smiles and waves: no stay of execution today.

'Let's see what we can do for you, January.'

He shines a light in her eye so bright that it threatens retinal flash.

'The eyes are the gateway to the soul.'

And the brain. Blinded like this she can hardly make out the certificates on the wall: perhaps third in pie-dish arranging, participation in a mini-triathlon and Quack of the Year three times running.

Robert draws squares in vivid blue all over her arms: she is a crossword and he doesn't have a clue. He drops liquid into each square and waits for a reaction.

He hangs specimen bottles of food around her neck and pushes down on her arms to see which weakens her.

'Well, this is very interesting. There doesn't seem to be a physical trigger. Has your eczema been this bad before?'

'Second year at uni.'

'And what happened then?'

Now that the ghosting in her eyes has faded, Robert's seem more intense than before.

'Just relax and tell me what happened.'

January tries to corral her thoughts into an orderly queue but, now the gates are open, they have all rushed to the front. She sighs and starts again.

January remembers her second year at university …

It is hard to keep her head above water; she is outclassed by everyone around her. They're better read, have opinions about things, and have no problem challenging the lecturers. If you can barely keep up with the readings, how on earth can you have an opinion on them?

Navigating the junk shop is never easy: a wrong turn and the path would be blocked by a stack of old records or a box of lighting fixtures. Often the paths would narrow off so quickly that a wanderer would have to back up slowly, aware that each step could set off an avalanche of old magazines and plastic collectables. On the nose of an old mannequin, she sees a pair of wire-framed glasses: an old display pair with clear glass instead of lenses.

If you don't have intelligence you can certainly fake it: wearing glasses, sonnets learnt by rote so that quotes can be sprinkled in conversation ... or simply not conversing at all, so that there will be no proof of your ignorance.

The rash starts behind her right ear, following the curves of the frame. The delicate skin cracks and oozes, caking the end of the glasses in dried yellow plasma crystals that catch the light. She wants to scratch, but the fear that if she does she'll be called upon to comment, her scratch mistaken for a raised hand, keeps her fingers at bay. Then they would all know that she is just average; that her sparkling wit is a heavily practised facade.

She hates her body for rebelling against her, trying to expose her true character. It had taken to her contrivances like they were an ill-fitting shoe, leaving her rubbed raw and bleeding.

The rash worsens the more she fights against herself. It snakes down her ear to the back of her neck, encircling her throat red and angry, like the hands of a jealous lover. It curves further still to her waist; constricting it with dry, scaly skin. Her body has hidden the itch between layers of skin. If she could run her fingers over her body without scratching, she would be able to feel the thick patches of eczema. Her calves are so raw with the itch that her socks and stockings have to be soaked off lest she rip the skin afresh. Her skin is taut, like it no longer fits: like she no longer fits. She wants to shed herself and be done with it.

The wind whips up the sand, momentarily replacing her itch with pain. She is the only person glad of winter at this moment. The cold air rushes around her, numbing her nerves into submission. She takes off her boots, her hat, her scarf, and walks into the water. Her skirt, heavy with water, wraps around her legs. She gives up the image of her elegant walk into the sea, and lets herself fall. The salt stings her skin and her eyes, but the icy water brings back some sanity.

Home again, she stands under the hot water of the shower, her skin crackling as the heat of each drop of water sends pins and needles through her.

Her life had to change. Three days later she became January.

Robert *hmms* like he's waiting for a prompt from the wings.

'I bet that it feels better to have it out in the open. Sometimes if we bottle up emotions they can be as dangerous as a virus to the immune system.'

She's not sure what she expected of Robert: a huge sigh, a look of surprise, a *Tell me about your mother* in a strange Austrian accent? Something to acknowledge the story she told him. Instead, he looks like she has just told him what the breakfast specials are – engaged but not very interested.

He breaks his gaze and writes up his notes. January doesn't know what to focus on now. Her head pounds and her mouth is dry.

'Drink this.'

She sniffs it, and takes a sip.

'It's water.'

'Of course it is, January. I'm not in the business of drugging people.'

How about hypnotising them?

'Well, January,' Robert has obviously studied TV doctors intently; he has the manner down pat, 'I've drawn a couple of conclusions from your notes. Firstly, I think you should avoid wheat: the dark circles under your eyes tell me that your body does not process gluten well. But aside from all that, your main problem is in here.' Robert taps his head with his forefinger, and January is surprised that there is no hollow ring. 'You live too much in your own little world. Ignoring reality will not make it go away.'

January stands. 'Look, just give me a cream or a pill or whatever.'

'That won't help.' Robert sighs and looks at his shelves. He takes a small bottle in his hand and presses it into January's. 'This will ease the itch and prevent infection, but it won't cure you. January, you need to be honest, at the very least with yourself. You need something, a goal to be travelling towards. You are stuck in the middle of nowhere with four flat tyres and one spare: you can't choose which to fix so you just sit there and wait. Remember the law of inertia. Get up and walk January, it is the only way out.'

Inertia. That is her biggest problem, inertia? The thought bugs her as she punches in her PIN and annoys her even more when Robert's orange face (blue, blue eyes and white, white teeth) wishes her a good day. Inertia: what kind of diagnosis is that? January watches her toes as her feet land in front of her. She imagines her leg swinging from her hip like a pendulum in a high school experiment.

A body in motion stays in motion.

January wonders if she should keep walking, past work, up the hill that winds through university all the way home. She has an illness and a cereal packet certificate to prove it.

seven

The card is conspicuous on January's desk because of the lack of anything around it. People like Alice can't seem to settle without their things around them, but January has never intended to settle. The act of claiming her space would imply that she intends to stay, even though the months turned into years a long while ago. The toys, the artwork, the photos all say something about their owners. It seems like too much trouble to January to find things that reflect her personality, when she isn't sure herself who she is. Perhaps, then, a conundrum like this card is perfect. She has stared at the little faces for a long time, willing them to divulge their purpose and meaning, but so far their lips have stayed fixed in their cherry-coloured smiles. When she can no longer stand their mocking looks, she turns the card over and stares at the inscription, tracing every letter to try and decipher a clue.

January's desk is ill-equipped for writing anything by hand; it takes a few minutes to find a pen and a trip to the printer to get paper. The paper, too big and too white for her thoughts, is ripped in half. She starts off doodling, drawing a border around her page and cross-hatching in it. Her hand cramps. Unused to holding a pen, she has held it too hard; her ring finger is indented and purple where the pen rested.

Reply in handwriting to ...

To what? Should she write about the grass, the sky, the day? Should she write about the children: imagine their lives as they are or as they will be? She looks at their faces and pulls her own face to match theirs. They giggle at her attempt: *Silly grown-ups and their funny faces!*

Children this happy don't exist any more. There are no longer games, just well-rounded activities. January cannot remember a time when she laughed as freely; when she didn't feel burdened with life's hopes and worries.

Tell me a secret.

The answer, once she thinks of it, is so obvious. Her hand scuttles crab-like across the page; she writes quickly to try and capture her thoughts. Happiness has always been elusive prey.

When I was nineteen I decided to change my name ...

A young girl waits outside a building of mirrored glass and concrete. Today will be her birthday of sorts. She knows that she cannot change her actual birthday, but today will be marked as the day when she became a woman of her own making. The foolish spend their life in self-reflection; she has found a faster and easier way of becoming a better person. All she needs to do is to change a few syllables: just the few grunts and sighs of language that tie her to her current life.

She has stood outside the building for half an hour now, unsure why she hesitates. For a building concerned with every part of your life – Births, Deaths and Marriages – it is stark and sterile. Life, it seems, does not sully this facade. If only she was that impervious. It is fitting that this rebirth be sterile: a clean start, a clean slate.

Tabula rasa: the only Latin she knows.

She is a blight; her reflection smudges the building. She could be anyone right now, her look is so indistinct. She has tried for so long to be different, and has only succeeded in becoming a drone, a watered-down caricature of the people who really live like this: Goths. She could only ever dip her toes in the lifestyle: reading the Romantics in the graveyard, drinking faux absinthe. The thought of actual death scares her; she couldn't bring herself to play at it every day. The long black skirt barely touching the tops of her boots (paint splatters optional), which are laced so that they are able to be ripped open in an emergency leaving the leather intact; the kohl-rimmed eyes; the vintage jacket that only allows a glimpse of her hands; the fingers ringed by the green shadow of copper-based jewellery. She threw it all away when she realised that this is not who she is, not who she wants to be. She chews the ragged ends of her nails, the black varnish chipped halfway down the nail bed.

It is time.

She walks into the building. Her reflection follows closely behind, and the building is wiped clean of her image.

This will be the last time she will say her name. In her low-slung bag, jostling with text books and a ragged romance novel, is a small jar wrapped in a silk scarf. It will capture her last breath before she is renewed. She had found it in an op shop: ten cents for an old baby food jar. Appropriate, she thought, for a new beginning. The fates must have agreed, because the lady at the shop had waved away the payment: *Just take it, my dear.*

The receptionist eyes her wearily as she opens the jar and carefully spells her name, ensuring each letter drops into the glass.

'Your name: it's what ties you here, it's who you are.'

But the girl doesn't want it. She doesn't want her ties. She wants freedom, she wants anonymity. No history to remember, no future to live up to. She wants life on her terms.

Three days earlier she had walked into the sea and as the salt stung her eyes she could finally see. Three days she had spent alone in her room, drifting in and out of sleep. On the third day she rose, and knew with absolute clarity what she had to do.

And no well-meaning woman, glaring at her over her glasses, will dissuade her.

'I know what I'm doing.'

It takes a couple of hundred dollars and a few forms to become January: a name of beginnings and ends, a name that looks forward as it looks back. If she were to look back, January would see that each step she has taken is like a fray in a thick rope. The fibres that had twined together, strengthened each other, finally unravel and snap. With the last official stamp she is cut off from her history. She has become weightless, anchorless. She is free now to make her own ties with the world: connections that she chooses.

January walks down the Terrace towards Parliament. The city has been renewed in her eyes and she feels at peace, perhaps even happy. The eczema that had driven her mad until three days ago has totally cleared, proving that this was the right thing to do. She needed to shed her old life to be happy.

The ghosts of the Bolton Street cemetery call to her as she walks past, recognising kindred: another who gave up her history to thrive in this city. January ignores them. She has fought to become this blank canvas; a woman who can pick and choose her ghosts. Her old superstitions still haunt her: she spits on her hands as she walks past Seddon's memorial. Her new life has lost a little of its shine as she settles into it: it feels so familiar.

January stops in the rose garden, barren at this time of year, the pampered bushes manicured to within an inch of their lives. The scrappy miniatures at the perimeter are the only ones left with any flowers: a few buds and orange hips. It seems so right; gathering from these forgotten little things always stuck on the outside, a fitting tribute. She covertly picks a hardy bud and hides it up her sleeve, then casually walks on, up and over the hill, past the controlled main gates to her tree. She sits in the arms of the tree, opens her romance and waits. Waits until the mothers take their young children home for their naps. Waits until the prepubescent groups cut through on their way home. Waits until the students walk into the wilder parts of the garden to surreptitiously attend to weeds of a different sort. Waits until the suits try to relax after a hard day with a pleasant walk through 'nature'. January waits until twilight masks the final ritual of her old life; or perhaps it is the first ritual of her new life.

At the base of her tree: an oak old and strong, strong enough to be a guardian, January digs a small hole with an old serving spoon. She takes the jar from her bag, places the rose bud on top and wraps it with the silk scarf. With a final kiss, she lays the bundle in the hole and covers it. She wipes her grimy hands on her skirt before she searches in her bag once again, this time retrieving a small flask of vodka. Her first tie has been made. She toasts: to beginnings and endings; to new and to old; to whet the baby's head and as a wake: a sip for the tree and a sip for January.

She feels like she has drunk too much. Her emotions have become crazy and uncontrollable; she feels as if she could cry at any second, even though there is nothing to cry about. This is exactly what she wanted.

I am happy!

January's mind protests against the tears that run down her cheeks. It just doesn't make sense to be upset. She refuses to allow herself the time to mourn. Determined to celebrate, she stomps into town, into a bar where they won't give a second glance to her grimy hands and make-up smudged eyes. Where if she told them what she had done today it wouldn't warrant a reply. This is the place where January is truly born: a place of shadows and anonymity. Where people sit together to be alone. She sits here until the lights go on and the barman cleans around her. She waits until his back is turned before she swipes a bottle of anything from behind the bar and bursts out the back door, running back to her flat, swigging raspberry cordial until it dribbles down her chin.

eight

A post-box slot angles up slightly so that a posted letter is protected from the elements. It is also protected from those who change their minds, the angle making it impossible to see your letter, never mind reach it. January knows as soon as she lets the letter drop from her fingers that she'll have to find another way to get it back. Soon it will be collected, franked and on its way to the address on the card.

Not that she signed it, or even gave a return address, but she let enough information slip. A stranger, a complete stranger, will now know things about her. She could bribe the postman, or she could drop a match in and immolate the lot. Or she could wait in the post office for her letter to be delivered.

The automatic door of the post office swooshes open. From her vantage point January can see the private box with only a slight tilt to her head. The takeaway coffee she holds is cold, but she sips it anyway: it makes her look casual, like she has business here. *Not that kind of business*, she thinks as she looks across the street to the trompe l'eoil hooker painted on a building. A painted lady indeed.

She should walk away: accept that she's never going to meet the person she sent the letter to and it doesn't really matter if she gives up now. This plan was never practical: the post box might not be checked today, or tomorrow.

Five rows across and six up: no one has cleared it yet. It is stupid to keep waiting. If the letter is that important she should write a note and ask for it to be sent back to her. January scrawls a note on the back of her business card, the first she's ever used, and slides it into the private box. She turns to leave and almost walks into an old woman.

'Excuse me?'

'Sorry?'

'My mailbox, you're in front of it dear.'

Her chance has arrived in a classic camel-hair coat and a woollen beret, and January does not know what to do. It would be so easy to ask for the letter back, but something stays her tongue.

'Are you all right dear?'

'Hmm? What? Fine.'

January can see the envelope between the old woman's gloved fingers. It would be simple to take the letter, but something stays her hand.

'All right then. Ta ta.'

Is it a complicated thing to follow the woman home? January's feet don't seem to think so, and they start their journey long before her mind has a chance to debate the ethics of the choice.

The woman lives in a little cottage surrounded by offices and apartments, and somehow its negative space makes it seem more imposing. The weatherboards have been painted green, but so many years ago that they have faded, and now have a greyish cast. The window that she can see is trimmed in red; the sills are white. The front door has been stripped bare, as if someone had decided to repaint it long ago and then lost the urge. The roof and the sides of the house are clad in galvanised corrugated iron, interrupted only occasionally by errant windows. On the left-hand side of the house is a word spray-painted in pure white, the letters large and round almost looped into themselves. The cottage is surrounded by a metal fence, no doubt protecting it from the outside world, but giving the impression that it needs to be caged, that it is dangerous. A house like this in the middle of the city, stand-alone with a small garden: why, if it got loose it might spread.

January traces her fingers over the spray-painted word – *Revolution* – enjoying the pling-plong sound as her nails hit the peaks and valleys of the iron. The rain that falls adds subtle percussion to her piece, until the gods decide that it is time for a drum solo.

The door swings open and the old woman peers out.

'Are you going to stand out there all night?'

January pushes herself hard against the wall, willing herself to be two-dimensional: a cunning rendering and nothing more.

The woman's voice is stern, but there is something else underneath that January can't put her finger on.

'I can tell you now that I don't have any fancy do-dads; any of those DCD players. Try another house.'

She's afraid. Afraid of me?

January steps out from the wall. She slouches, trying to look as pathetic as possible, which, being completely wet – hair dripping and make-up running – is not that hard to achieve.

'I ... I don't want ...'

January looks down at her shoes, ruined by the puddle she's standing in.

'What do you want?'

'It's hard to explain.'

'You could try explaining to the police why you're lurking outside a defenceless old woman's house.'

'Please, I'm not going to hurt you.'

'Then go away.'

'I can't. I need ...'

'I've nothing stronger than a cup of tea.'

'I'm not a drunk.'

The woman, hands on hips, stares straight at January.

'You do realise it's raining, don't you?'

'I forgot my coat.'

January bites her lip and crosses her fingers behind her back. The woman looks her up and down.

'You'll catch your death if you stay out there, and I'll not have that on my conscience.'

The woman steps to the side of the door, allowing room for January to come in. She hesitates, the surprise of the invitation rooting her to the spot. 'I'm not asking you again.'

Drips from January's clothes hiss as they drip onto the fire. Huddled naked under the quilt that is tucked around her, she stares at her tea, trying to discern the feeling that churns in her stomach. It is almost like being home, like a part of her knows this place already. The mismatched filing cabinets in the hall, the overblown autographs framed on the wall and the piles of paper: a fire hazard stacked too closely to an open fire. Even the seat seems to embrace her. It is almost too much: it seems like if she got too comfortable she would never be able to leave.

A cat strolls into the room and circles the quilt pooling at January's feet, kneading and purring.

'What's the cat called?'

'Cat.'

Of its own accord January's left eyebrow arches.

'The curve of her back is like the spine of a 'C', the 'a' is her hunched body ready to spring upon a victim and her whiskers remind me of a 't'. 'Cat' seemed to be a good fit.'

Cat narrows her eyes in approval.

January imagines the letters traced over Cat's body with the cheesy fluorescent lettering used by kids' shows of the early eighties. C ... a ... t ...Yes, she can see it, but it has been a long time since that 'a' has been hunched for hunting. 'Coot' might be more appropriate. As in 'Old'.

'Thank you for the tea. I'll go as soon as my clothes dry; I bet you don't want a stranger in your home.'

'Yes, especially one who has followed me home. You're not a god-botherer are you? I'm not ready to make an appointment with him yet.'

'No, why would you think that?'

'Well, it's better than the other alternatives I came up with.'

'My name is January ...'

The mail sits on a small pile on the arm of the woman's chair. January can see the envelope under her hand.

'Ah, the letter.'

'Yes. I was wondering if I could have it back.'

The woman finds the letter and looks at it.

'Funny thing, I was going to send it back when I read your card, but now I say to myself: "Mae," – that's my name dear, very pleased to meet you – "Mae, this letter could be interesting!" After all, you've gone to all this trouble to get it back.'

January gulps her tea. She follows the envelope in Mae's hand until she feels sick with the motion.

'Then, my dear, I look at your face and I think: "Mae, you can't possibly let this poor girl suffer this way! Where is your mercy? Where is your soul?" But would humankind have ever progressed if the needs of the few outweighed those of the rest of society? This is important research, perhaps more important than the feelings of a half-sodden girl. It is a dilemma. What do you think of it, January?'

'I'd give it back.'

Mae's eyes narrow and her smile widens.

'Would you?'

'Yes. What do you need it for anyway?'

'Research: finding the depths of the human soul. Much more important than a little embarrassment, don't you think?'

'I didn't say I was embarrassed.'

'Yes, you did.' Mae flicks the business card to January.

'It just asks you to return my letter.'

'Yes, but it also says more. That and you turned bright pink when I mentioned the letter. Yet your dripping underwear in my parlour hardly raised any colour at all.'

January closes her eyes and rubs her neck. The harder she rubs the itchier it gets, until she is suddenly aware that her nails are leaving rake marks on her skin.

'You'll only make it worse worrying it.'

Great, just what I need: another nag in my life.

'Your problem, January, is that you over-think things. If you scratch the same spot over and over it just becomes infected; it doesn't go away.'

'What do you know about me, Mae?'

Mae raises an eyebrow and breaks the seal of the envelope.

'Please don't read it.'

'Who said anything about reading it?' Mae holds the letter upside down. 'Sometimes the words get in the way of what someone is really saying.'

'I find that a lot.'

Mae folds the letter and tucks it back into its envelope. 'I can see that.'

'How?'

'Did you not wonder, dear, why I wanted handwriting samples? I'm a graphologist; I explain the wonders of the human psyche through the art and the science of graphology.'

'I've never heard of graphology.'

'I'm not surprised. Graphologists have been relegated to the status of soothsayers and palm readers: parlour tricks to amuse the bored middle classes. But one doesn't need a crystal ball if the evidence is in front of you, plain as day.'

'Evidence of what?'

'Of personality, of the true self. Here, see for yourself.'

Mae moves across the room with surprising speed, locating two samples from the legion of papers stacked around the room. She hands them, triumphant, to January.

'Tell me what you see.'

January looks at the papers in her hand. One is filled with tiny writing; the other overflows with large letters that spill across sentences.

'Don't read them. Just tell me what you see.'

'One has small writing and the other is big.'

'What does that tell you?'

January suddenly feels as if she is at school again. Her answers curl up at the ends – questions themselves – searching to please the teacher.

'I guess to write this small you'd have to be patient, and maybe have an eye for detail …'

January looks up at Mae, who nods her head in approval.

'Maybe they'd be a bit shy: it's like their writing is shrinking away from me. But this one, this person doesn't care what the world thinks. The letters are so large it's like they're shouting at me.'

Mae takes the papers from January.

'That's what I do. Graphology in a nutshell.'

Mae places the samples back on their piles.

'You, by the way, did very well for your first time.'

Mae pours tea into both their cups. It has sat for so long it looks like Indian ink, and tastes not much better. January manages a gulp and looks around in vain for a plant to tip the rest into.

'And … my letter?'

'Do you want it back? Or do you just not want me to read it?'

Mae flicks it back and forth in her hand so quickly that it isn't a surprise when it lands in the middle of the fire.

'Oh, look at that. How silly of me. I must be more careful: important research and all that.'

'Thank you.'

'There is one thing I'd like to know. Why did you change your name, January?'

nine

Rain is easy to love if you don't have to go anywhere and can stay wrapped up in bed with a book and a warm cup of tea. It can be invigorating to be caught in the rain, soaked to the bone on the way home, where a hot shower awaits. The sound your clothes make as you peel them off; the slurp and plop of them as they drop to the bathroom floor before the heat of the water drills holes in the numbness of your limbs, covering you with a pleasant pins and needles tingle.

The buses have been filled this week because of the rain. People who normally eschew public transport are jammed into the aisles with only the tension of their bodies to hold them up as the bus lurches from stop to stop.

The bus driver guns it between every stop, braking at the last possible moment. January's bag throws her off balance and into the man in front of her yet again.

'Sorry.'

A little bit of January isn't really. Every lurch is an excuse to feel the texture of his coat; damp and scratchy. To be pressed this close with a stranger is quite erotic. The heat of their bodies steams up the windows; the warm smell of damp clothes musts the air. She closes her eyes and suddenly she can feel the pressure of his lips against hers, a kiss so urgent that her teeth rip her lip's soft tissue, coating their tongues with blood …

'Excuse me, Miss? This is my stop.'

Typical. He gets off before January is even warmed up.

It is a short run between the stop and her flat, but she still feels breathless. The shock of the cold, fresh air clamps her lungs down to half their capacity, making her pant with every step. January battles against the weather to close the front door. She leans against it and slowly slides down.

'Drink!'

A shot glass of syrupy yellow liquid is shoved into her hand. The girlfriend wears an off-the-shoulder peasant blouse and long black skirt.

'I forgot the salt and lime! Hold on.'

January takes her drink into the lounge, trying not to spill it. Her flatmate sits on the couch, a sombrero on his head and a moustache drawn on with black pen.

'Tequila!'

He obviously started well before January got home. The girlfriend appears with a tray of corn chips and lime.

'I hope you like Mexican, January, because tonight is fiesta night.'

'Friday Fiesta!'

'Ah, ah, ah! Español, baby.'

January places her shot glass on the table, where is it is immediately claimed by her flatmate.

'My Spanish teacher said the best way to learn is to be immersed in it, and since we can't afford it – well not yet, eh hon?'

'Si.'

'… We thought we'd bring Mexico to us.'

'Si. Señor.'

'"…ita". It's "señorita," babe.'

The girlfriend pours out three more shots. January stares at hers as they lick, swig and share a wedge of lime. Their smacking kiss is more stomach-churning than the cheap tequila on offer.

'Actually, I have plans.'

It takes a second for them to remember that January is still in the room.

'I'm visiting a friend ... in town.'

January walks out of the room, and picks up her bag at the front door. The tequila makes their voices carry.

'But I cooked and everything.'

'Don't worry babe. She's one loco señorita.'

The girlfriend's giggles are mercifully drowned out by the rain.

The cottage lit by the street light looks as if the rain has washed away the last remnants of colour. It is a ghost of a former time, its cast iron side a suture for its long lost twin. At one time the cottage was one of many, built shoulder to shoulder. Workers lived there, families. Slowly each was eaten up by development: a road, an office block and eventually apartment buildings. It is a hole in the landscape; an oasis of the antiquated.

Some people would look at this dilapidated cottage and think five storeys; ten tops. A block of land this big in the middle of the city is a property developer's wet dream.

Wet all right.

This is the second time she has stood dripping wet on this front step. Last time, she missed the small sign nailed by the door.

Graphologist.

Mae Raine.

January's laugh is refracted in the puddles around her; it's typical of her to seek shelter in the Raine.

Her knock on the door reverberates as if the cottage were hollow.

'Mae? It's me, January.'

No lights, no movement.

January presses her face against the window, but it is impossible to see anything without the lights on. What if Mae has been hurt and is lying dead on the floor?

She picks up Cat, who is meowing at her feet. *Well, I guess you'd be fatter if that were the case.*

'Would she leave you all alone?'

Alice is January's only reference when it comes to cats, and she speaks to hers with puffed cheeks and pouted lips, adding extra 'o's and 'w's to her words. Cat's ears flatten.

'Fair enough, it annoys me too.'

Cat struggles in January's grasp; a nip to the arm and she is free; landing neatly at January's feet. January rubs her arm, more from shock than hurt.

She follows Cat down past the corrugated wall, tracing the graffiti – *Revolution* – with her hand. She follows Cat over the fence and into the small back yard of the cottage, praying that no one in the apartment buildings is watching. Cat disappears through a cat door and January sits next to it, glad for the little shelter the back porch gives. Cat pops out again and looks at her.

What are you doing, you stupid human? My food is in here! Anyone can get through. I measured it myself, and these whiskers don't lie.

'What are the chances, Cat?'

January lifts up the doormat.

'Not very good, it would seem.'

January kneels down and peers through the cat door.

'Mae? Are you home?'

Cat licks January's hands and meows.

'Cat seems really hungry. Mae? Are you all right?'

January dumps the contents of her handbag on the ground and her penlight almost rolls away. She twists it on, but there is no light. She smacks it against her hand like she has seen in the movies. Nothing. She twists the end off her torch and pulls the dead batteries out. She hopes it is not too late for mouth to mouth; she's not sure why it works, but a little chew seems to perk batteries up. Each bite down sends slivers of pain down her teeth, paralysing her jaw for a second. She hopes that she doesn't bite down too hard and release acid into her mouth; she needs that juice for …

The light from the torch does not flood; it is barely a drop, but it is sufficient enough to see the lock on the inside of the door, once she has figured out the angle to hold her pocket mirror. She lies on her back; her head is wedged against the door and her arms are through the cat door. Awkward, but she has the patience for this kind of puzzle. The lock is a simple push-button; twist the inside door knob and it will be released. She stuffs her empty bag through the cat door and flicks the strap at the door. All she needs to do is hook it around the knob and pull it taut. The strap slipping off the round knob would spell failure, but she is sure that the width of the strap will compensate for that. It takes a while to hook, working blind and backwards, but she finally succeeds, and with a firm pull the door opens. Give a girl a pen knife, some duct tape and a mullet and she can do anything.

'Mae?'

The cottage is dark and cold. She bumps into a pile of paper in the hall. The light from the street casts strange shadows, and she gropes for a light switch. She hesitates. If Mae is dead does she really want to see it? Then again, wouldn't it be worse to trip over and end up face to face on the floor?

Click.

Even though she is blinded by sudden light, January can see Mae is not home. Cat weaves around her legs.

'I had to break in, to save you from starving.'

January follows Cat to the kitchen, which is neat but small and seems to be the only room not overflowing with paper. But it is overflowing with cat food in an automatic feeder.

'Liar.'

Cat eats, happy for the company; her purrs drowned out by the rain on the iron roof. January peers outside; the rain is heavier than when she arrived. There's no harm waiting out the storm; at least she could have a cup of tea and let her clothes dry a bit.

The cottage is filled with the rattle of the kettle boiling. It clicks off, and then steam rises from the tea pot as the leaves unfurl and colour the water.

She lights a small fire as the tea brews. The rain drills holes in the silence.

Cat has already claimed her spot by the fire by the time January returns with her tea. She wraps herself in a quilt and looks at light flickering around her, the flames reflected over and over by the frames on the walls. Warmth envelopes her; the hard lines of the walls soften like cotton washed again and again. Mae and her tea are forgotten, abandoned thoughts razed by the fire.

Perhaps this could be the place where they can be alone together. The cottage is a poor cousin compared with his yellow house, but somehow it makes it seem more authentic. This place is not concerned with stature and the facade of wealth; here the passion and love are real. This is the place where he will choose – rather than feel obligated – to be.

Cat nudges the strange girl's hand, but she is too limp with sleep to scratch Cat behind the ears. Cat settles into her spot by the fire, her purrs overlapping with the girl's soft snores.

The city falls away. It had only been a theatre flat, a poorly rendered facsimile, grotesque and out of proportion up close, but real enough to the people in the audience. In the place of buildings, the cottage is surrounded by magnificent trees, including January's tree just outside the back door. Its leaves shelter her alabaster skin against the heat and light when she reads here in the afternoon. She raises her hand to shield her eyes from the sun. It is high; he will be here soon. She will not be taken advantage of; she rehearses her refusal, shaking her pretty head, her glossy ringlets swinging like bells chiming: 'No, no, no, no'.

Every day since he first brought her here, it has become harder to refuse. Three days earlier they had quarrelled and she, flushed and frustrated, had turned away from him and started home. She curses herself for being so hard-headed; his proposal had been ... adequate. In a moment his strong hands had encircled her and lifted her onto his horse, taking her away from the world she had known.

You will learn to love me!

He declared it with such force that she had fainted, and awoken many hours later, intact, in the cottage.

If only he knew how I already truly love him.

But his wanton act of stealing her away has hardened her heart against him. Her reputation is surely in tatters, despite her determination to keep the affair unconsummated. She has nothing to feel shame for, but it would be she who would bear the brunt of judgement when they returned to society. If they returned. She simply cannot leave until he does the right thing by her; however long it takes she is prepared to wait.

She has come to love the cottage: her room upstairs with the ceiling sloped in harmony with the roof, the fireplace cosy and warm in the dark silent night. He is taking good care of her, bringing her fresh food each day, books to stave off boredom. In the afternoon, he strips off his shirt and chops wood for her. She spies at him through her window, admiring the restrained power of his muscles as they easily swing against the logs. It is at this time her resolve is at its weakest, and she secretly longs for him to take her in his arms, still glistening with sweat, and crush her will with his lips. It is a bitter-sweet blessing when he mounts his horse and leaves without a word of goodbye, his form constricted once again by shirt-tails and jacket, for if he looked back she is sure that she would beg him to stay.

In the still of the forest she can hear his approach, the gallop of hooves mimicking her heart beating in her breast. Try as she might, she cannot quell the excitement of his return.

In a moment he arrives. He swings off his horse, hot and sweaty after his long ride. His lips burn with barely restrained passion against her offered hand. Her looks up at her with eyes that burn, his desire barely kept in check. A smile curls the corners of his mouth, and she blushes as she imagines his lips on hers.

'My lady …'

Cat lands on January's lap and she is startled back into this cottage, the real cottage. Mae's cottage. The fire has burned down to embers, yet Mae has not returned. Probably won't for a few days at least: the cat feeder is proof of that. There's no point in moving now: the buses have long since stopped and the rain sounds as if it has no plans to.

'Just until the morning, Cat.'

ten

A morning of meagre light and bird song; the rain behind it is like the hiss of a speaker. The traffic sluices the street, stirring the slough that has formed in the night. A fire engine screams past, and January remembers the fire. But it went out a long time ago, just like Cat, even though January is still folded awkwardly to accommodate her claws. The chair seems too small for her now, the damp of last night swelling her joints. The hunch in her back returns as she tightens the quilt around her. Old age is not biological but architectural; the chair has sapped some precious life from her. She shuffles to the kitchen, stretching her fingers around a mug, hoping the warm tea will chase away the cold exhaustion that haunts her.

She sorts through the mail on the kitchen table, which has not been opened since she was last here, feeling the weight of each envelope: some heavy and thick with their contents waiting to blurt out, some thin and unsubstantial, barely a whisper. She looks at the quality of the paper, the addresses that are held so tightly that they have become a part of the paper's fibre, the rejected addresses; slipping slowly down. And she looks at the return addresses: they are not all from this city. How many cards has Mae pinned up around the country, maybe even the world? Somewhere another person may be looking at the same small postcard she did. Somewhere someone else is deciding to reply.

January's business card falls out from the pile. It is small and insignificant compared with the rest, and she regrets now the absence of her letter; it speaks worse of her than what she had written. What would Mae have known from January's letter? She had only glanced at it before tossing it in the fire.

January erases herself from the cottage: washing her mug, replacing the quilt. The pile of papers she knocked over will be more difficult – who knows what sort of system Mae uses to sort her collection, if there is a system at all. Mae's home is a museum of writing: she is an avid collector of all – random scribbles, crumpled notes and discarded deposit slips, crossed out and corrected. This is a love affair with the written word: the written word, not the printed word. Handwriting in all its forms: legible, illegible, large, small, measured and relaxed.

The cottage's plain walls are adorned with autographs blown up to monstrous sizes, pinned and framed like ink butterflies. These and the piles of paper represent personalities summarised by a few lines and squiggles. They whisper secrets that January cannot hear. Although she can guess at what the messy sample in her hand says about the author, it is just a guess. Even if they were here now – hands shaken and tea shared – anything she knew about them would be a guess.

There are several books on graphology on Mae's shelves, but none of them with the beginner graphologist in mind. January pulls a large encyclopaedia down from a shelf and dislodges a small leather-bound notebook. The cover is worn but still supple, the edges and spine darkened by the sweat of hands. The pages have begun to yellow. The writing inside is small and precise: so perfect that it could have been typed.

The first page bares a simple inscription:

A Graphologist's Life.
M Raine.

She should close it and put it back on the shelf: she has stayed here too long already. But January does not, cannot replace the book; she is compelled to read on.

The tools of a graphologist are simple and few; most items will already be available in most households – a ruler, a fountain pen, a sharpened pencil and a sharpened mind.

Cat sticks a sharpened claw into January's leg. She snaps the book shut and Cat withdraws her threat.

'I'm only borrowing it. I'll return it when I come and check on you.'

The space the notebook leaves on the shelf is as conspicuous as this very cottage in the city. She pulls the romance from her bag to stop the gap, and from a distance it is not a bad stand-in. The notebook fits snugly into the hardcover shell, protected from the ephemera in her bag. Taking the spare key is a simple choice, any moral or even legal qualm outweighed by January's obligation to return the book and, of course, her concern for Cat.

It is a slow walk home: the weekend shopping crowd meander on the street despite the weather. January lets herself be carried along with them, noticing the subtle differences in expressions or gait. She follows one woman whose clipped walk makes January think of Mae's writing – meticulous and sharp.

A sharpened pencil and a sharpened mind ...

Mae's words in January's mind are punctuated by the woman's heels clicking on concrete and then on tile as she walks through the threshold of a department store. January's feet halt despite the door being held open for her, the doorman's friendly welcome rarely matched by the women who work inside. She turns away, hoping that the doorman won't take it as an affront, and she is almost free when the display in the window draws her back.

Pens all colours and shapes, bright and cheerful, classic and traditional. Some worth a month of her rent. She imagines holding a pen like that and wonders if it would improve her writing. Such a pen would demand you have something to say. January doesn't think she has anything worth saying.

January gives a small nod of thanks to the doorman, who winks in return.

Under the lights of the cabinet small pots of ink are displayed. It looks red, like blood. Ink for signing diabolical contracts; to sign your soul away.

'It's love letter ink.' Sales assistants have a nasty habit of sneaking up on you. She opens the cabinet with a key – these pens are so precious – and takes out a bottle. January rocks the bottle gently under the light, marvelling at the colour.

'It is scented with roses too.'

January hardly notices as she is lead by the elbow to a desk.

'Here, sit. Would you like to try it?'

Before January can answer the woman has taken the bottle from her hands and broken the seal. Clever, now January will feel obliged to buy it. Although she would probably feel obliged to buy it anyway. January always feels sorry for them, stuck in shops all day. Temptation all around them.

The woman dips a fountain pen into the ink: once, twice. Smiling, she hands the pen to January. January can almost feel the hunger for the sale radiating from her hands.

The pen is heavy and warm. She has never held a fountain pen before. The page before her is blank, and so is her mind.

'What should I write?'

'Anything. Just try it.'

The only thing that she can think of is her name. Slowly and deliberately she forms the letters, the nib scratching the paper. This feels more permanent than writing in ballpoint. Ballpoints allow you to speed across the page, unconsciously filling the void. With a fountain you have the time to think about what you say. January is awed at the beauty of a letter, the gentle curve of her 'a'. She takes pains to perfect the tails of her 'J' and 'y'. Her name has become a thing of joy.

'Can you smell the roses?'

January can, and her name has been transformed into something sublime, a holy relic. She traces the letters of her name, feeling the small indent created by the nib. It is a tattoo on the paper.

Her hand has been marked as well: an ink blot spread across her ring finger where she held the pen too low. She knows she will buy the pen; already her hand misses the weight of it. The ink that has seeped into her skin, bright red like blood, has bound her to it.

'Do you sell notebooks as well?'

eleven

A Graphologist's Life.
M Raine.

The tools of a graphologist are simple and few; most items will already be available in most households — a ruler, a fountain pen, a sharpened pencil and a sharpened mind. It is deceptive, this short list. It has fooled people, tricked them into thinking that all they need is a pen and a cipher to claim to be a handwriting expert. Though the tools may be simple, the art is anything but.

Over the many years that I have been a practising graphologist, I have valued one tool above all others. It is a tool that cannot be picked up for a few cents at any stationer; it is a tool that is regrettably missing in many households today; it is a skill that some have a particular knack for, and in which some are sadly wanting.

It is the gift of empathy.

The capacity to identify with others is the cornerstone of the art. A graphologist must be able to 'walk a mile in another man's shoes'. A graphologist must know how each letter is formed by his subject — each muscle contraction and pain in his arm, the pressure the subject exerts on himself and his pen. To this end, a novice must spend a good deal of time tracing his collected writing samples until every twitch and quirk of penmanship has seeped into his being.

A novice must learn, too, when intuition must stop and objective observation must take over: application of the rigorous procedure that separates the graphologist from the fairground charlatan; for graphology is a science as well as an art.

Empathy and observation are the guides the graphologist must rely on, in the knowledge that these principles have guided many others' journeys before.

My own journey started a lifetime ago. I would love to tell you, dear reader, that it was a deep-seated desire to understand my fellow man that spurred me on this journey, but alas, the truth is far more mundane. Like so many other human endeavours, my journey started with love.

And, like many of those other stories, the love was unrequited. He was married, in more than one sense: a wife back home in the United Kingdom and his work as a graphologist here. His research was fascinating; a man's handwriting, like his character, is formed by his environment. There had already been some research into the 'American hand' — their letters stretching over the page like their wide prairies. He was curious to see the Antipodean hand — how our landscape pulls our thoughts across the page. He must have thought it paradise to come to the capital: the natural harbour and the hills, the people slanted against the wind, their coats as black as ink spots. He would sits for hours at a time crouched over his samples. There were times I fancied that if I ran my fingertips down his spine I could read his thoughts as the blind do Braille.

But ours was not that kind of relationship. In the beginning I was hired to type his notes — his hand was unreadable by design. I was a quick student, able to decipher his writing in an afternoon, where other girls had taken at least a week.

Other girls: later on the thought of them would tighten my shoulder blades like a laced corset. Had the other girls listened so intently? Had the other girls taken an interest in his ideas? Had the other girls proven to be so adept?

It was he who first recognised my talent for interpretation and steered me toward what would turn out to be my vocation. I didn't realise the lessons he taught me at first. Bringing order to the samples he collected seemed simply secretarial; sorting paper into piles according to size, spacing and slant was self-evident. Later, when I began my study in earnest, classification was second nature to me. Procedure was not something I had to learn — it was innate.

The ease with which I learnt is a gift I wish I could give to you, dear reader. Unfortunately, teaching is not counted among my talents. So bear with my clumsy attempts to impart my knowledge to you. Like a child with a pencil too small for his grip, I am untrained and unformed.

You have gathered your tools and your material. Perhaps you have cleared a space to work, or have promised a friend that you'll reveal their secrets. You are itching to start, but I am urging you to wait. Some, no doubt, have already skipped ahead, too eager to heed a gentle word of caution from the author. Indeed, that type of person regularly ignores caution, letting it slip from their fingers at the slightest stir of a breeze. One day, too late perhaps, they will find their way back to my words of warning.

I am offering you a choice. I fell into graphology: fell into traps carefully laid by my teacher, and although I do not regret my life, it would be irresponsible for me to lead you as blindly.

Think back, if you will, to a time when you could not read: when letters were indecipherable themselves, let alone in a string called a word; a cord called a sentence; a rope called a book. For most (save those of you with a photographic memory, which must be as much of a curse as it is a blessing), this will be an impossible task. Was there really a time when you could not read just at a glance? When the world was so closed to you? What did the world look like then, uncoloured by the words and thoughts of others?

When you begin (and you will, dear reader, indulge me a little longer), you will be like that child again — struggling to form words, hands cramped from writing the same word over and over, the world once again closed to you. But do you really want it open? One day, it will be as natural to you as reading, as unconscious as breathing, as part of you as any other of your senses. Every letter, every card, every hastily written note will be naked to you: the shape of letters, their slope down the page will speak more to you than the sentiments written. Are you prepared to learn what your friends really think of you, or the way your mother feels about her life? Do you really wish to seek the truth?

How many of you, dear readers, have I lost now, either to impatience or to blessed ignorance? How many more will drift away? How many will stay true?

For those who have made it this far, welcome. I hope you are prepared for the arduous journey ahead: an odyssey, if you will, into humanity. I cannot promise you that all you will see will please you, but I guarantee it will be the truth, and what more can we really hope for?

Let us dive right in, as they say, at the deep end. Take a breath to prepare and we'll jump in together. Ready?

Let me tell you ...

twelve

Let me tell you about my ghosts. Not the Dickensian kind, tormenting me for a life lived selfishly, nor the kind that come knock-knocking at your door at the twitch of a monkey's paw. My ghosts have been my secret, the secret, the reason that I can see what others cannot. Perhaps now I am ready to share it.

A tap at the window disturbs Mae's train of thought, and she looks up. Hanging on to the carriage window, stretched and straining against the speed of the train, is a ghost. Mae waves at it, and it waves back, its mouth turning into a great 'o' of surprise as it loses its grip and the train rushes ahead. It springs backwards like elastic giving on a satin slip: there is nothing to do but let it pool at your feet and continue walking, a forgotten piece of yourself abandoned on a city street. Mae looks back and waves again, and the ghost limply replies in kind. Her attention turns again to the paper in front of her.

How can I begin to describe them? In the past, I have been hesitant. I justified it to myself, claiming that it would be like trying to describe a colour to the blind. I could say that blue was the crisp cold of metal against skin, biting in winter and a relief in summer. It is the smooth chill that almost feels wet to the fingertips; it is mint and watermelon on the tongue. But words are inadequate, the concept of colour itself is impossible to define.

Let me begin my description with an assurance that I am not some sort of witch, trapping souls within the confines of paper prisons. Nor am I a medium, reading the séance crowd and impressing them with cheap illusions. In the simplest way, when I analyse writing, I conjure a person. Not a facsimile, but a true personality. Once it has gotten over the shock of sudden existence, the whispering begins. Of hopes lost and cherished, of lies told, of little perversions. I simply listen and write.

The ghosts made of little more than ego cling to me. Their only tie to this world is my willingness to listen. The problem is that once life is given, most creatures are reluctant to give it up, including, it would seem, the non-corporeal. They clog my stairs and hang in the rafters, their incessant whispers keeping me awake at night. If I am lucky, a southerly pummels the city and I open my doors, allowing the wind to rent them apart. But it is horrific to witness their tenuous grip on the world rupture violently, so I prefer the method I'm employing now: the silent escape. It is akin to putting a crayfish in the freezer before tossing it into a pot of boiling water. The lack of scraping against the pot allows you to fool yourself that it does not hurt. That it is a humane way to kill.

In a few days I will return to a cottage that is free of them. I won't have to witness their slow expiration, their very being dissolving from lack of attention.

I often wonder what it is like. Cat is mildly horrified when I arrive home, smothering me with rabid attention and kisses. But that is, perhaps, due to the automatic feeder's lack of fire-making ability. Her hollow threat of feasting on my mortal remains is not because I abandoned them, but because I abandoned her. For all I know the ghosts could disappear the instant that I'm gone.

The click of Mae's pen lid is a full stop. She will write no more tonight. The light already fades as the train climbs up the country. Mae stretches her fingers: kept supple, she believes, by the exercises she continues to do. In her youth, horrified by the haberdasher's humps she saw fusing some women's backs into rigid arcades, she had devised a regime of stretching and calisthenics.

The state of the body reflects the state of the mind: a supple body is a supple mind.

One last note before daylight has gone completely. Mae binds her notes into a simple leather wallet. They are working documents: a title which always amuses Mae as it seems that she is the one that works and not they. She will pare down her thoughts: whittle away the unnecessary until her points are sharp. Only then will it be transcribed to her journal. The train bisects the country, ruling a straight line that brings order to the chaotic countryside, which is a patchwork of paddocks and crops stitched together with windbreaks and fences. The rhythm of the movement and sound, like a giant mechanical heartbeat, reminds Mae of the lines she used to rule as an apprentice.

Shick. Shick.

Squared out from the side, even lines a quarter of an inch apart.

A sharpened pencil and a sharpened mind.

Trapped by her pencil lines, the samples became like curiosities at a zoo – the predators stalking up and down the page, looking for their chance to pounce; the skittish fading behind their bars, glad for protection at last; the attention-seekers basking in the light. Mae had thought it a cruel thing to do, but it made it easier to examine their form, their size and their slope; and in time as her eye became keen, she could observe them at a distance.

Mae rubs her neck, watching the country speed behind her. Wellington, her cottage and Cat are now far away. She needed a few days out of the city. She needed to come home. The familiar squall of excitement and apprehension stirs in her stomach. A cup of tea would calm it, but she is so close to home that she decides to wait. It is the same every time she visits. She used to reason that it was the thinning air as the train climbed further and further past sea level, or that it was motion sickness brought on by the scenery whizzing by. What she knows now is that it is the land welcoming her back; it will nourish her for a few days before the pull of the outside world becomes too strong. Each time she visits, the urge to leave becomes weaker and weaker, and she knows that some time soon the land will refuse to let her go. She will be landlocked, buried next to the family she left behind.

The walk from the station to her house is fairly short – much shorter than the walk from the station to her cottage in the city – but tonight it seems longer, as if the space between each house slows down her walk. She had thought she had lost the slow gait of a true local years ago, replacing it with a prim trot: the side-stepping dart needed to navigate the city. The rhythm of this place always loosens her stride: her legs swing a little easier from her hips.

Mae avoids the hotel, wanting, for once, to sneak home anonymously: to have one night alone with her memories. Her childhood home has been preserved like it is her own private museum. The windows that rattle in their frames when it is windy, the old iron bed head, the heavy woollen blankets as comforting now as they ever were when she was a child. She clings to the water-colour memory of that time, an indistinct representation of what it was really like: the artist only frames the picturesque.

The Raine house sits apart from the others on the hill, overlooking the town. Mae climbs the path to her door, her journey made easier by the light from her home. She has been found out.

'We would have picked you up Mae: you just had to call.'

Mae sets her suitcase down and removes her coat and gloves. The newly made fire crackles with the excitement of existence. She rubs her hands together in front of its warmth.

'I don't like to be a bother, Cheryl.'

'It's not a bother, Mae. It's more of a bother to me when you walk home.'

'I walk home all the time in the city.'

'Well at least there'd be people around to help you if you fell over there. What would happen here if you hurt yourself? No one would know you were out there, would they? You might have spent the night outside in the cold.'

'Well, obviously someone knew I was here, otherwise you wouldn't be here.'

'Jimmy saw you get off the train and called me.'

The kettle whistles and Cheryl warms the teapot.

'You know all you have to do is call me and I'll pick you up. And you should have stopped in for a drink at the hotel. People will be hurt that you didn't say hello.'

Cheryl clutches her cup of tea, and takes a big gulp. Mae rubs Cheryl's arm.

'I'm sorry I didn't call, Cheryl.'

'I just worry about you being all alone. And look at this place, it's a tip. I would have cleaned up if I had known …'

The house is spotless and smells of beeswax and lavender. Underneath that creeps another familiar smell, the damp dog smell of impending rain, its arrival felt by joist and joint.

'And I bet you haven't eaten yet. I didn't even bring any bread.'

'I'm fine; I was going to head for bed soon.'

'Do you feel all right? You haven't caught a chill, have you?'

'Just tired.'

Cheryl attempts to check Mae's temperature with her hand, but Mae catches it in her own.

'I'm fine, Cheryl.'

'I'm just worried about you. I've been thinking. You should come home and I'll take care of you.'

'And the kids? And Jimmy?'

'They won't mind.'

'Well, I guess it wouldn't be for very long anyway …'

'Mae!' Cheryl covers her mouth in surprise.

'Gallows humour, my darling. If I don't laugh I'll cry, and you'll be doing enough of that for the both of us.'

Mae burrows deeper into her bed, hiding from the cold that seeps through the cracks of the wooden floors and walls and somehow cannot find its way out again. The hot water bottle at her feet is not Cat, who despite her wriggling and snoring makes a better bed companion than the bladder of water slowly turning cold.

Had the tap at her door not been just slightly out of time with the raindrops, Mae might not have heard it. Although she would have heard the thump of small feet that followed it and felt the weight of the child who sat next to her.

'Mae? Are you dead?'

'What sort of question is that?'

'Mummy said that I had to be quiet 'cos you were dead to the word.'

'World, dear.'

'So I wanted to ask you.'

Mae sits up in bed and places one palm against her forehead and the other on the child's. She swaps hands so quickly that she slaps her own forehead. Jasmine's laughter is a mixture of delight and surprise.

'Not dead. Not yet anyway.'

'Good. 'Cos I have a present for you.'

Jasmine is out of the room long enough for Mae to pull on her dressing gown and slippers. She returns with a drawing: bright spring-like forms curve over the page. Mae cannot help but recognise Jasmine's traits in her picture – her good humour and curiosity.

'Thank you, Jasmine. I have something for you.'

Mae opens a tin of sweets bought especially for her visit. Jasmine takes a handful, stuffing some into her mouth and the rest in her pocket for later.

'I'd like a cup of tea, how about you?'

'Hey lady!'

Their little noses are pressed hard against the window, smudging out the view with their hot breath.

'Hey lady!'

The only flowers here are the sad carnations half shrivelled in the white bucket out the front. Mae would like to leave them, but she can't go empty handed.

'Hey! Lady!'

Twenty years ago, maybe more, it would have been their parents: dirty-nosed kids begging for sugar.

Hey lady! Can you get us a twenty-cent mixture?

Now a dollar barely gets the same amount. When she's feeling particularly nostalgic, Mae doles out the lollies one by one and tells them what the world was like when she was their age. They stare at her incredulously when she tells them what you could get for a dollar then.

Bet you could buy a car too! Did you even have cars then? Or did you ride around on dinosaurs eh?

The whole town seems to be out today. A few days of rain and it looks like the whole place has caught cabin fever.

A few of the older locals raise their eyebrows in recognition.

'Miss Raine! Thought you were home.'

'Bush telegraph working overtime?'

'Nah.' He points to the sky. 'You always bring it with you. Birds of a feather, eh?'

The same old joke. Mae doesn't know how many times she's heard it in her life. It used to annoy her, the look of triumph on the face of the comedian, convinced that they had come up with a fresh witticism, but now it makes her feel as if she is really home.

'Maybe I should visit more often: I don't want to cause a drought.'

'Remember you can have too much of a good thing, Miss Raine.'

'In all my years, I've never found that to be true.'

Mae dances away, splashing the puddles at her feet like a child. She nods to the locals as she passes, picking up speed on the way to the cemetery. She has bones to visit before her train ride back to the city.

She holds out her hand expecting rain, fooled by the staccato of the tap. The cemetery is overgrown in places. The forgotten ones: their people have long moved on from this place. There are a few new spots – here and there an earth mound that hasn't sunk, marked by a makeshift white cross and a plastic flower whose petals catch the wind and spin.

Mae runs her hands over the simple black granite, shiny from the rain. She had, for a moment, considered an overblown mausoleum, angels atop heralding heaven, but her father would have hated that much attention. He was a humble man, and this seemed more fitting.

She lays the flowers down and kisses her fingertips, pressing love into the cold stone. She traces their names, cut deep into it:

Walter and Hazel Raine, beloved Father and Mother of Mae.

These ghosts stay put in their graves, content to be part of her memories rather than haunting her life.

Farewells, no matter how practised you become, are never easy. Cheryl cries as if she'll never see Mae again, and tries to refuse the extra money Mae presses into her hand.

'Take it, for all the bother I've put you through this week.'

'I don't need it, Mae. You pay me more than enough for the little cleaning I do for you. You're like family …'

Mae leaves her standing on the platform, knowing that it is better to be done with it than to let it drag out. She glances back as the train chugs forward, and for a moment she thinks she sees in Cheryl's wave goodbye her father, hat off and heart-broken. She turns her head forward like she had so many years ago, so he wouldn't see her tears.

thirteen

The handwritten note and memo had been a rarity even in Mae's time as a novice, when the business day had already become measured by the clang of a typewriter. Now, the wealth of samples – personal letters, lists, even deposit slips – has long since disappeared into the digital void.

January has scavenged a meagre collection of samples. She sorts through recycling, her eye as keen as a magpie for any flash of writing. The method has not borne much fruit.

She could send around an email and ask for samples; she is sure she'd get a few that way. But she imagines the interest each person will take in her project as they drop off their sample; their awkward hope that she will reveal their true genius and the obligation she will feel to tell them something. That email will never be composed.

The photocopier sheds little light on January's predicament. This has become a daily ritual. The hum of the scanner and the smell of the warm toner clears her mind to be as blank as the paper the machine so ruthlessly brands. She hesitated at first to copy Mae's journal, afraid that its delicate spine would break under the weight of the photocopier's lid. Practicality won out; January had no idea when Mae would come back, and copying her work by hand might take weeks or months, if she tried to mimic Mae's writing precisely.

She had tried writing it in her own handwriting but somehow it didn't feel right, as if her own hand was not authoritative enough. She cranks up the contrast on the next page, hoping the print will come out dark enough to trace; killing a couple of birds with one well-aimed stone. At least she has Mae's writing to practice with: slow, precise and measured. Her body has begun to reflect her study, not just in the hunch in her back, which needs regular stretching to be released, but also in her gait: her stride has slowed and each step is precise, as if her feet scribe a perfectly straight line.

She places her new pages in the back of a folder already bulging with pages waiting to be transcribed. The page she is currently working on sits on her copy holder, obscuring the work she is supposed to be doing. Her desk is like the cottage in miniature, housing piles of paper she is sorting according to Mae's classification system. She has interesting samples pinned to her cubicle walls – the originals and the blown-up photocopies jostle for space. There is an area left clear for transcribing, or perhaps in the future for analysing samples.

Her desk is all dressed up with nothing to do.

She needs a sampler of writing, like those big boxes of biscuits that are around at Christmas time: a variety of little tastes. Perhaps she could start a petition – that wouldn't seem out of character, she's always complaining about something – but it would only give her signatures, and they are too small a morsel.

Her fountain pen has become as familiar as her hand; it is almost a part of her. As hand and pen move together across the page, it is difficult to discern where one ends and one starts, particularly as the ink has stained her fingers to the same shade as the pen's barrel.

> *Sometimes, it is advisable for the graphologist to down tools and to forget about their studies; visit friends, go to the pictures or perhaps take a short break away. Most often a solution to a frustrating*

problem will present itself while our minds are occupied with pleasures. I encourage the novice to take some time for themselves, to stretch their legs if they will, for how can one expect to understand life if one does not live it?

And it is true. In the queue at the stationers her mind is on her bank balance – carefully calculating each of the days between her last pay and now, each coffee and lunch she has bought, each cent carried over and whether the remainder will be enough for the ink in her hand – when the solution, garish and oversized, catches her eye.

'Leaving card for Ted.'

January holds out the card and a pen and her co-worker, the man she thinks of as Limpy, takes it from her.

'You're collecting for Ted?'

'Yup.'

'Where's Alice?'

'Busy. Do you want to sign?'

His hand is true to his being: his greeting lurches across the page. January has impressed herself with this idea: it is the perfect way to collect samples. Not only do you get the writing, but you can see your subject in situ. She has half a mind to write a little note about it in Mae's journal, her own contribution to the art. But she is getting ahead of herself: she has more samples to collect. Each inscription in the card is a tributary filling her pool.

'It's for Ted ...'

'I know who you mean. The guy with the bright ties, that's Ted, right?'

'Right.'

Uses a pencil – afraid to leave a permanent mark perhaps? A little left-leaning and messy, like the pasta sauce stain on his shirt.

'When's his party?'

'He wants just to leave quietly: a sad time for his family, y'know.'

This one barely scratches her name on the card, her letters dropping downwards like her limp hair and running mascara.

'I know Ted, good bloke. Where's he off to?'

'Don't know. A better job I guess. Maybe he's retiring.'

'Nice for some eh?'

Over-sized letters and placement right in the middle of the page: he is expansive and talks with his hands.

'Why are you doing this? You hate Ted.' A1's eyes narrow over the top of the oversized card.

'No, I don't.' January knew it was a mistake to come to reception, but she had to know if A1's writing was as angular as her body.

'Whatever, dork.'

She signs *Best wishes*, dotting her 'i' with a small heart, and January vomits a little in her mouth.

The real and most elusive prize for January is Alice. She just can't ask Alice to sign the card: as president of the social club, it would usually be Alice's job to organise it.

'Where have you been, January?'

'Just talking to a couple of people …'

'For your report?'

'… yes.'

It's not really a lie: she *is* working on a report, and Alice did not specify what report she meant. January tries to tuck the card away before Alice sees it.

'What's that?'

'Ted's leaving card. I thought I'd, um, help.'

Alice sighs. Of all the times January could be helpful, she chooses now. 'What am I supposed to do with this?'

Alice holds an identical card to January's and laughs.

'Look, most of these people signed both the cards. They didn't even notice ... it's sad: it's like Ted doesn't even matter.'

Alice does not know why she is suddenly upset. Perhaps it is guilt: she has been counting the days until Ted leaves. Counting the days until she gets the job. If she gets the job.

Applications close ...

Today, Alice had been relieved that January had kept herself busy this morning so that she could concentrate on her cover letter. She reads it and feels pleased: she has plenty to offer. She's loyal, hard-working. She knows the company inside and out. She gets on with everyone in the department (the Ana twins notwithstanding) and knows that her experience in self-actualisation could benefit many people in this company. She includes her ideas for team-building and self-esteem courses in her letter: it is what she is passionate about.

Based on this letter, she thinks she has a pretty good chance. Maybe even a better chance than January. If she applied. Of course she'll apply. Alice feels the confidence drain out of her like pasta water in a colander when she thinks about January applying. Of course they'd pick January over her. January has a degree, which would be a big plus.

January's attitude to work and to life in general make Alice despair. It is as if January thinks the whole world owes her something, so instead of making an effort in anything she waits for the world to provide. It is so frustrating that January has the potential to do something with her life but is too lazy to grab it.

God, she wants this promotion badly.

Alice chews her lip in frustration, transferring creamy pink lipstick to her front teeth, a fact she will be unconscious of until the twins mock her mercilessly for it later. Not knowing will drive Alice crazy.

'Are you applying for Ted's job?'

'Maybe. If Ted can do it I guess anyone can. I haven't really thought about it.'

'Applications close today.'

'I guess not then.'

Alice's smile bursts into a genuine grin. A strange sense of relief relaxes January, as if she was a chocolate éclair at a diabetics' convention: she is safe from the ravenous jaws. At ease once more, she opens her journal and begins transcribing where she left off.

CONNECTIVE FORMS
Perhaps the most telling of all features of handwriting is the way in which a person connects one letter to another. These connections, to the trained eye, can reveal how a subject relates to the world: they represent a bridge between the subject's ego and others around him.

January raises her head over the cubicle divide. She looks at Alice's desk, festooned with pictures and with her computer positioned so that others are welcome in her space. There is no reason to think her writing would be any different. The firm, rounded garland of a gregarious woman: her strokes would imitate the wide and ready smile that often wrinkles her eyes.

But it is a frown that wrinkles them now.

'Can I help you, January?' The slope in Alice's voice is at odds with her sentiment.

'No, I'm just going out for a smoke.'

'I don't know why you keep doing that to yourself. It is the slowest form of suicide you know.'

'Should I get myself a shot gun and just be done with it?'

'You may as well: at least then you won't be a burden on the health system.'

'What is this, tough love?'

Alice sighs. 'Don't you have any respect for yourself?'

January would like to say *Apparently not*, each syllable curled with the plummy accent of radio announcers past. She imagines rising from her desk, her scarf flung over her shoulder and her hair moved by an unknown breeze, then sweeping from the room, leaving Alice dumbfounded at her desk. Reality, as ever, disappoints. She gathers her bag and creeps out of the room, with the shame of being – a smoker? No, just the shame of *being* clings to her hair like day-old smoke.

You would think that Alice would give up, but perhaps nagging someone about smoking is just as addictive as the habit itself. January read somewhere that the pictures of gangrenous bodies they print on cigarette packets did not turn people off the habit. Instead the sight of the sores made a smoker crave the nicotine more, the terrible images somehow mixed up in the pleasure centres of the brain. If she really was a smoker, would Alice's words of warning just become a kind of foreplay for her; something that made her desire stronger?

January shudders at the thought of foreplay with Alice. It's enough to make you quit. And that is what January intends to do, with a little help from Alice.

Alice is so focused on her screen that it takes two sighs before she pops her head over their divide to investigate. Perfectly staged, January is slumped over her desk, her coat still on, her head buried in her arm, her packet of cigarettes in her hand.

'January?'

'I just couldn't do it.' A slight sob to her voice, but not enough to be unbelievable. 'I just couldn't. Everything you said just kept going around and around my head.'

Alice walks around and kneels beside her. She can feel Alice's hand on her arm. Her head snaps up and she forces the cigarettes into Alice's hand.

'Take them: rip them up. I can't do it myself.'

Alice breaks a cigarette in two, and then another. A small yelp from January accompanies each break, making it seem to Alice as if she is assaulting them.

'Are you sure this is what you want to do?'

'I was out there and I began to think about what you said about suicide, and I dropped my smoke over the edge and for a moment it looked as if it was me falling. It made me feel dizzy and I had to come back in. I don't know what I'm going to do, Alice, quitting is just too hard.'

'If there is anything I could do …'

January clasps Alice's hand. 'You've already done so much. It was your words that inspired me to stop. I just hope I can remember them when the withdrawal kicks in …'

'You could call me.'

'In the middle of the night? It wouldn't be fair. I don't want to be a burden. If I had your words of encouragement with me always then it wouldn't seem as hopeless.'

'I'll jot them down for you.'

January smiles. 'Here, borrow my pen.'

fourteen

Mae waits out the worst of the rain at the station, eventually buying an umbrella for the short walk home. A waste of time and money in this city really; even those who have spent many years perfecting the tricks of fighting the wind will admit there are days when it is better to let the rain soak through you than to fight against it. Those days when the rubbish bins overflow with the skeletons of dead umbrellas, killed by a squall that snuck up from behind and popped them inside out.

She would have been better off spending the money on a taxi – at least then she would have had a chance of getting home dry, but she cannot abide all that fuss for such a short trip. The walk home gives her time to adjust her rhythm back to the city; she wouldn't be able to function if she was out of sync. Her strides tighten and shorten; her step becomes swift. The wind shifts, and she throws the handle of the umbrella over her shoulder. At this time of the night it is quiet. The city has gone home from work, and it is too early for the drunks to emerge. It is the perfect time for a meditative walk.

Mae likes to walk down out-of-the-way alley ways on the way home, to check what graffiti has grown since she has been gone, like a gardener tending young shoots. She is devastated when the council obliterate her crop: water blasting or, worse, commissioning a mural to beautify the area. The tags are treated with ignorance. Someone with a voice tells the media that the perpetrators have no respect for property and no pride in themselves. They are accused of committing a thoughtless act.

This is a misinterpretation: there is respect, there is pride, there is thought. Can they not see the stylised angularity of a person desperate to be taken seriously, who wants the world to see them? The letters are unintelligible to the outsider, like the mumbled responses of a sullen teenager; the meaning of them invisible to those blind to it. Could they, in good conscience, punish someone for speaking in a language foreign to them? She should have taught more people: at least given them the basics so that their world view would not be so narrow.

The graffiti on Mae's wall has survived because of her love for it. The word and the act are incongruous to the personality that wrote it. Mae wishes that she had caught them; not to punish but to question. Why 'Revolution'? Is it something you believe in, or the only thing you could think of? She would have invited them in for a cup of tea and asked why they picked up the spray can in the first place. Was it a dare? Or was it done to prove something to someone by the usually considerate and well-mannered author? Perhaps she would have shown them her graphology books, inspired another to learn; inspired a different kind of revolution.

Cat is waiting on the doorstep when Mae arrives, and greets her with a purr and an arch of her back. Why Cat waits at this door to be let in when she has a perfectly good cat door out the back is a mystery. She impatiently stands on Mae's toes as she turns the key in the lock and races ahead of Mae to the kitchen, the prospect of fresh food too tempting to wait for removal of coats and hats. She looks back at Mae, still at the door, still in her coat and hat. Her hands are out as if she is balancing herself, as if the whole world has shifted slightly to the left.

Mae closes the door behind her and creeps down the hall. The rows of filing cabinets and piles of paper are still there, but the hem of her coat no longer disturbs them. She walks backwards to the door again, retracing her steps like a novice unsure of his interpretation. She has not been this hesitant since that time. She has only been away a short while: her memory must be playing tricks on her. A cup of tea will ground her again.

The kettle is barely under the tap before it overflows. Mae tips the water out: a cup of tea should never be made with stale water. Usually she'd empty the kettle before she left. She must be getting old and forgetful. She has even forgotten to turn on the lights; she is creeping around her house like a burglar. Her hand has frozen above the light switch before her mind comprehends what she has just seen. A movement at the back fence: not Cat, who is chewing her food noisily at Mae's feet. It is a shape that is too big for a cat in her back yard: a shape that is coming towards the kitchen door. Should she flick on the light now and hope that it frightens the person off? Or would that simply aggravate someone intent on breaking in? Mae expects the glass to break, not the sound of a key easing into the lock and smoothly opening it.

'Hello, Cat! It's just me.'

A female voice. Mae looks at Cat, who is feigning ignorance by cleaning her tail.

'Conspirator.' The hiss in Mae's voice scares Cat under the table.

The light is switched on, and January is blinded. Through squinted eyes she can make out a figure before her.

'Leave now, before I call the cops.'

'Well, that would be interesting, a burglar calling the police.'

'Mae? It's me, January.'

'I know who you are, just not why you're here. With my spare key, I might add.'

'I was checking on Cat. I was worried that you left her alone.'

'With plenty of food and water.'

'I didn't know that before I broke in. For all I knew you were dead on the floor.'

'Am I supposed to be reassured by that? Why did you come back?'

January pulls Mae's journal from her bag, and Mae snatches it away before January's ink-stained fingers can cause any more damage.

'What are you doing with this?'

'I wanted to learn. I thought you could … teach me?'

'Leave.'

'I've already started, Mae.' January digs through her bag again. 'I have a few notes that you might like to look at.'

'Please leave now.'

If this was a movie, Mae would change her mind before January reaches the door. She would call January's name and they'd make up over a cup of tea.

'January.'

January smiles at Mae, but it is not returned.

'The key.'

Mae clutches her journal to her chest as if she is trying to still the beat of her heart with the weight of it. She can see January's intrusion everywhere, her inky fingerprints smudging the air around her. What else has she sullied with her indiscriminate hands – the piles of samples beside Mae's desk or the other volumes of her work?

She began the journal a lifetime ago as an attempt to capture her thoughts so she could make sense of it all. The first entries were lost, deliberately, some time ago. The original pages were too naked and vulnerable, as unformed and undisciplined as their author. Those first pages, written in the peaks and valleys of an over-emotional school girl, eventually replaced by tight observations written in an equally tight hand.

What would Mae make of her now, that girl who has been lost to time? Would there be a clue in her script that hinted at this future?

Her work, her *life* has not seemed so vulnerable until today. She had trained her hand so that she would reveal nothing of herself, except perhaps to a master. Her secret assured by the unwillingness of others to learn. Mae's attempts at teaching had been frustrated by the lack of commitment of her students. They only wanted to find out whether their partner was cheating, or to be placated with their own superficial personality traits; that their writing marked them out as intelligent or kind. None wanted to push their studies or the science further, and Mae had given up on teaching them. She concentrated her techniques and thoughts in her journal instead.

She holds the battered romance in her hand as she replaces the journal on the shelf. January had wanted to learn: she could hear that in her voice. Her writing had suggested some intelligence, and breaking in shows some commitment. Can larceny ever be a good testimonial? No, she cannot risk the disappointment of another failed student; she doesn't have the time to waste. If only she had kept the letter January had sent, then she could get a real idea of the kind of woman she was dealing with.

January's only hope of reprieve was destroyed the night they first met.

fifteen

There is a rash forming in the crook of January's elbow. It feels hot and raw as she scratches, rubbing the fabric of her sleeve against it like it is sandpaper.

'Say I did something to you, Alice. Do you think you could forgive me?'

'Depends what it was, I suppose.'

'Something that was kind of an accident; something I didn't mean to do.'

Alice checks that everything is still in order at her desk: it is; including Chairman Meow sitting at attention next to her computer.

'A cup of coffee would do me, January.'

'It's something a cup of coffee won't fix.'

'What have you done?'

'Don't worry. It's nothing.'

But Alice is worried; she checks her drawers, her files, the shared drive and the report she's been working on. Nothing is amiss or out of place; everything looks normal. She looks at her daily mantra to slow her breathing down.

Life is not always as it seems.

It is a sign, a sign! Alice begins her checks again.

January's morning has been quiet. Concerned for Alice's health, she had popped her head over the cubicle wall to see if she was all right. Alice was busy searching through files, her brows pinched together by her frown. Too busy to prattle on about finding her authentic life, too busy to gossip about the cellulite-pocked thighs of celebrities. Too busy then to help January with her problem: finding a way to make Mae forgive her.

The problem was that January didn't really think that Mae should have taken offence. She had the best intentions when she broke in; if not to save Mae than at least her cat. Perhaps she should have left when she saw that everything was fine. Perhaps she should have left the journal on the shelf. It was breaking and entering, but not in the classical sense; she had always intended to bring the journal back. She had copied the journal word for word into her notebook: not just the words' meaning but also their form. She had spent her days at work and her nights at home clutching her fountain pen tightly, replicating Mae's definite strokes, her photocopies as reference. This way she has come to know Mae, not just through Mae's words, but through the ache in January's forearm and the ink marks on her fingers. At least, she *thought* she had come to know Mae; that she would be flattered for the attention, that she would want to teach January all her secrets. The problem was that Mae didn't live up to her journal. She was not how January thought she'd be.

She opens her copy of the journal, and although it says the same things; it doesn't feel right – the pages are too heavy, as if they are overburdened with words. The answer must be in here somewhere. She is tempted to stick a pin in the pages and read a passage at random, hoping that the accidentally found wisdom would be applicable. Instead, she starts from the beginning, her eyes scanning down the page looking for something: anything, a clue.

> *Clues to a life are abandoned every day. The hastily written note, the deposit slip, the autograph, or, most telling of all, the random*

doodle; to the trained eye these reveal a person's hopes, fears and life itself. These forgotten ephemerae are a goldmine for the student of graphology, allowing access to a wide range of samples without the subject's intrusive involvement. However, a student would be wise to approach these samples with caution – they cannot be a true representation of personality because of their brevity. It is preferable to find a sample of two to three pages in length – but where can the novice find such samples? Faced with the same dilemma many years ago, I devised a plan to have samples sent to me – often by complete strangers. I like to think of it as a fishing expedition, and the bait is a simple greeting card.

Is the way to a graphologist's heart handwriting samples? Will Mae's heart soften when she collects the samples from her mail box? Each one will be addressed to January, so Mae will know who is responsible for her good fortune; to whom she should be grateful. Births, deaths, marriages, birthdays, congratulations and commiserations; anything of note, any occasion upon which you'd send a card; January looks for them all. The newspaper ink blackens her fingers as she searches, line by line, in the classifieds. It is quite possibly the most random task that she will ever do: sending out cards to anyone – royalty and celebrities, politicians and newsmakers – in the hope that she may receive at the very least an autograph, or, if the gods are smiling, a handwritten note in return.

How many cards has Mae sent out over the years? The task seemed overwhelming until January decided to focus on only one aspect of life – death. An apple a day keeps the doctor away, but what keeps the grim reaper at bay? Nothing, it would seem; in a week he would collect enough souls to fill this office from this city alone. January has begun looking at her co-workers through funereal eyes. What would their obituaries say? *A1, survived by her shadow, has finally achieved her goal of the ultimate tan, having been found shrivelled like a raisin in her tanning bed. Friends say it is the thinnest she's ever been …*

What would January's say?

Her spreadsheet is filling up after only a few days of searching the obituaries. The smell of newsprint is exciting and sad, the thrill of finding a possible candidate tempered by the thought that a life can be reduced to a few printed lines on a throwaway piece of paper.

Death is becoming an obsession, sinking into her skin and stinking on her breath. January can see the slow decay of humanity around her: the coughs of the diseased and the marks of the aged. She reads about the many ways in which a life can be snuffed out and she writes a list: a spell of sorts to keep the horror of mortality at bay.

> *Random ways in which you could die.*
> 1. *The headache from which you are suffering turns out to be a brain aneurism and not a head cold coming on. On top of that you have wasted $15 on a cold and flu remedy.*
> 2. *A car ploughs through a pedestrian crossing. I saw that happen to a woman on Abel Smith Street. She was all right, but maybe you won't be so lucky.*
> 3. *You could be hit by lightning. The nylon socks you wore are now fused to your feet. Those novelty socks won't seem so funny in eternity.*
> 4. *Not listening to your mother, you eat as you walk. You choke on a piece of chocolate bar, a peanut. No one stops to help because they are rushed too. Everyone eats on the run. It saves time. How much time have you saved?*
> 5. *You could be walking along Lambton Quay when the big one hits. The land once reclaimed by the city is now taken back by the sea. You drown in the backwash from Petone.*

6. A piece of debris falls through the ceiling of your office and kills you. Or maybe it flies through the window. Or maybe you're at home. Any which way, you're dead.
7. Spontaneous combustion. Enough said.
8. The chicken you ate at lunch gives you semolina ...

Alice's head appears at January's shoulder.
'I think the word you are looking for is "salmonella".'
With a jolt, January minimises her screen. Her work pops up.
'Hard at work, I see?'
'I was just taking a break, Alice.'
'You seem to have been on a break for the past week. All you do is read the paper ...'
'I like to be well informed.'
'Well, here's some information for you. I won't cover for you any more, January.'
'Cover?'
'Yes, cover. People have noticed ...'
'What people? It's just you and me, Alice.'
Alice walks back to her desk and leans on the cubicle divide.
'You need to stop thinking just of yourself.'
January opens her list again as Alice lowers herself into her chair. If she knew how January's thoughts had been occupied by other people recently would she still criticise? It is all that January has thought of since Mae threw her out. It seems like a lifetime ago: actually, precisely twenty lifetimes, according to her list. Of course there have been more – many more than the handful January has settled on – but these were the lives prominent enough that a card from a stranger would not seem out of place; prominent enough for a letter of thanks to be sent to those kind enough to send their sympathy.

She really needs to send the cards today: the names she collected earlier in the week will soon be interred; a card received then would seem a little odd. She folds her list of names and places them in her bag.

She peers over the divide. Alice has gone. Her absence makes January straighten up like an exclamation mark; if she is quick enough, perhaps Alice won't even notice she's gone. She is almost at the lifts when Alice appears, holding a fresh cup of coffee. The acrid smell makes January's nose wrinkle into a sneeze.

'Where are you off to?'

January speaks to the static image of Chairman Meow. 'I have a few things to do.'

'None of which are work, I guess.'

Chairman Meow's eyes are slits, awaiting a response that she knows will be met with disapproval.

'I won't be long.'

'Take as long as long as you like. It wouldn't make a difference anyway.'

Alice's voice is as hard as the porcelain mug that disappears from January's view, and January is left with the same queasy feeling as drinking coffee on an empty stomach.

Buying cards for people you know is hard enough, but when you are buying cards for names that you have gleaned from a paper the task becomes a Herculean nightmare. The sheer volume of cards is overwhelming. The counter has done a brisk trade with other customers before January decides to go for plain generic, clearing out the entire pocket on the shop's shelf.

She looks for a card for Mae, knowing exactly what she will say: a brief note asking to be taught. January has planned on using a little bait in her request – a few quirks of handwriting that she has already learnt: a rightward slope, a slight raise at the end of her sentences, a consistent and steady rhythm. She will be the perfect student: at least on paper. She chooses a card that reminds her of the card Mae had left at the supermarket. It is small with gold-tipped, scalloped edges; the border is embossed so you can feel the pattern under your fingertips, and the bouquet of red roses printed on the front looks as if it is a Victorian design.

It is almost closing time, and January has yet to make it to the counter. She has spent so long looking for the perfect card for Mae that she hasn't realised that the day has slipped away. Alice was angry enough with her when she left; imagine what she will be like now.

There is an entire stand of cards with cats. Maybe for cats; January is not quite sure. She has always been amazed at how deeply people feel about their cats. Alice is practically obsessed with Chairman Meow. She finds a card with an image that shares his same disapproving gaze. It is blank inside. January has no idea what she will write to fill it.

She climbs the stairs to the office, certain that Alice will have gone by now. It is quiet and dark. She dumps the cards on her desk and starts addressing them. It will probably take a couple of hours to do. At least she can pretend she made up her time after hours: she'll have her swipe card as proof.

The last card she writes is for Alice, and she is so exhausted that she can only manage one word:

Sorry.

sixteen

The red light on her phone blinks in time with the ring. January has stared at it since it began like it is some strange insect that's landed on her desk, its angry buzzing threatening to sting the hand that answers it.

'January speaking.'

'I'm not interested in playing games with you.'

'Mae? How did you get my number?'

'You wrote it on the card.'

'You got the card?'

'I don't know what you hoped to achieve ...'

'I want to learn, can't you see that?'

'Did you think I'd fall for it? Did you think I wouldn't know that you changed your writing?'

'Maybe.'

The receiver in her hand, an anchor that ties January to her chair, seems to lighten with Mae's laugh.

'The traits you chose were impressive, but that's what tripped you up. You can't cherry pick behaviours and throw them together higgledy piggledy.'

'I wanted to show you how much I've learnt – how much I want to learn.'

'Then show me something real.'

'What do you mean?'

'Graphology is more than memorising traits and tendencies. It is about understanding humanity. I want to know how you see the world, January. I want to know what you know about love.'

'Will you teach me, then?'

'We'll see. I'll expect your letter in the next post.'

January holds the lifeless beige receiver as if it was a parasite recently detached from her throbbing, red ear. What can she tell Mae about love?

Her fountain pen rests on her finger. Her dry skin sucks in the ink and it feathers and veins in the small cracks of her hands. There is more ink on her hands than on the page, which mocks her with its blankness – a perfect reflection of her mind.

She wishes now that she had something on her desk to look at, something that might inspire her. She digs through her bag and finds the latest romance. Would Mae know if she lifted a story? She could embellish it with things from her own life, so it would have an authentic feel. She begins to write and it flows easily. The usual characters: the wrong man, the right man and the woman torn between the two …

… A pair of earrings: globes of glass, scarlet, amber and gold, that seem to burn with their own fire, gold birds tucked in between the clusters of beads that hang suspended from the ear as if they had no weight at all.

They shone against her hair the night the right man saw her for the first time. She was illuminated on the dark path of the park by an old-fashioned lamp post, her arms wrapped around another man who kissed her neck passionately. Although her body was his, her mind was not, and she looked at the stars above as he bit into her.

Then, as if pulled by gravity, she locked eyes with Mr Right. Neither could look away: it was as if no one else existed in the world between them. Their gaze was suddenly broken as she was pushed against the lamp post violently. The right man rushed forward, but was stopped by her pleading eyes; he knew that he could not help her here. If this was affection what would abhorrence look like? She bit her lip as her inconsiderate lover ploughed deeper into her, and slid her earring out of her lobe. For a moment she was frightened that Mr Right would not understand, but she trusted that fate would not be as cruel as the man dragging her deeper into the trees. As she glanced back around and saw him, the right one, kneeling to pick it up and slowly follow her, she knew that this would all end tonight, one way or another …

January has written many pages before she notices her fingers are cramped and smudged. She wants to finish it off but her hand refuses, and her deadline looms. Perhaps Mae would enjoy reading it as a serial. She folds what she has into an envelope and puts it in the mail tray before the last of it is cleared for the day.

January doesn't know if it is her nerves or excitement that makes her want to pee. She has sat at her desk all morning, not wanting to move in case she misses the call from Mae. She concentrates on the tap of her foot, trying not to think of water or coffee. Mae should have got the letter this morning; January thought she would have rung …

The first ring is cut off by January's eager hand.

'January speaking …'

'I asked you for something real, not something that was ripped from a cheap paperback.'

She has no right of reply: Mae has hung up before she can even open her mouth.

She runs to the bathroom and locks herself in a stall. It is a funny sensation to be relieved and anxious at the same time.

The story had seemed so real to her. She felt every kiss, every thrust. She had imagined it so many times that she could remember herself there in his embrace: the weight of his arms, the cold lamp post digging into her back.

But Mae had seen through it; seen through her. January wonders if it was her writing that gave her away or the prose as purple as a day-old bruise. January wants to learn more of Mae's secrets, but she is unwilling to pay the price for them. Is it worth being so vulnerable to learn this so-called science? Why does she even care what the rest of humanity is like? She has survived years cut off from life. She scratches her arm. The rash has risen again, red and itchy. It seems in this moment that her life is festering inside of her; her secrets infecting her blood and making her skin sensitive to the world. Perhaps the naturopath was right; her pent-up emotions have begun to attack her physically. She should lance them like an over-ripe boil and let the truth ooze out. She will purge and cleanse.

'Are you all right in there?'

The knock on the stall brings her back to reality.

Back at her desk, January starts a new letter for Mae.

> *Late summer: the savings on daylight are running short. There are concerts in the Botanical Gardens, late strawberries and bubbles enjoyed by lovers picnicking on rugs. We sat on different rugs, he and I; he couldn't afford to be seen in public with me, even on our first date. We sat side by side, islands unto ourselves.*
>
> *I made earnest conversation with the grass I plucked strand by strand, relieved that I did not have to speak directly to him —*

if I looked at him my mouth would dry and the words would stall on the desert of my tongue.

As twilight fell the music ceased, and one by one the rugs were packed up and drifted away. Soon we were the only rugs left in a desolate ocean, each not wanting to move lest we broke our glorious isolation.

I shivered, my flimsy summer dress inadequate as the sun sank. As if on cue he pulled the rug around my shoulders, cupped my chin in his hand and looked into my eyes.

I felt faint under his gaze, like my body was just an encumbrance to my soul. My legs felt too light for the weight of my heart as he drew me up to my feet.

'Come with me. I have something to show you.'

We were flying. I could not feel the ground beneath my feet and the rug flapped behind me like a cape. In the darkness pin-pricks of blue light hung from the trees, as though each tree had been decorated in stars just for us. Under the fairy lights of the glow worms we kissed for the first time. I wished I could hold on to this moment forever, but we were caught short by a rabble of children and their minders. The glow worms' light display turned off in the wake of my echoing laughter as we ran from the crowd.

They glow only for us! Only for us!

We ran down the hill to a tree whose limbs were low enough to sit on. With surprising strength he swung me into the tree, hungrily kissing me. Cocooned in the rugs, we became lovers for the first time that night.

January puts down her pen, the ache in her body all too familiar. She has felt like this since that night. Their first date had set a precedent for the rest of their relationship. If you could call it that: she knows his arms will never be open to welcome her except in darkened alley ways and other clandestine rendezvous points. Some nights when she stares at the stars as he hungrily moves within her something in January tells her to hold on: that one day he will realise that he loves her. All she has to do is wait.

A classic enabler, Alice's books would say. January has created this relationship herself. It is she who has allowed herself to be treated this way, created the roles that they play. She has created her bed and now she must lie in it.

If only she had a bed with him, she would gladly lie there.

She stuffs her pages in the envelope, her mouth so dry that she needs to run her tongue over the seal twice. The address is messy with her rush to write it; January wants it in the box before she changes her mind. But her letter doesn't make the last post. Nor does it make the first in the morning. The envelope is sitting in her bin when Mae calls.

'I can't tell you about something I don't know, Mae.'

'You don't have to tell me anything at all, dear. It's your choice if you want me to teach you.'

'I'll send you something tomorrow.'

This time it is Mae who has no time to respond before January has rung off. Mae stares at the receiver, willing it to come to life before she gives up and replaces it on its cradle. It seems much longer than a few days since the arrival of January's plea to be taught, partly because of the steady stream of letters that has been arriving in Mae's letter box since then; all, curiously, addressed to January.

The little minx has used that old trick of mine.

Mae has collected them into a bundle and placed them near her desk, in a small space she has hopefully cleared for her new apprentice. The samples will sit there unopened until January's arrival. Mae is almost certain that there will be no letter from January waiting in the morning, but she can't stop that feeling of anticipation: the kind that preoccupies an adolescent mind awaiting a message from her crush.

The first letter from January had been a joy, despite the fact that it read like a tawdry bodice-ripper. Mae could see that she was trying; she could see something close to desperation in her words. She needed to push her, to test if she really wanted to learn. She had hoped that her test would encourage January, but maybe she has pushed too hard. Perhaps she has cleared a space in her life too soon.

She delays her walk to the post office an hour or two, waiting longer than usual to clear her private box, wanting to give a little extra time for her letter to arrive, even though she knows that the post office clears and delivers at the same time every day. She shuffles through the letters, searching for her own name, each 'January' a pinprick on her spine.

January has written the address with a firm hand, using the block capitals of a person anxious for their intention to be clear. Mae's pace quickens in anticipation of the secrets January's writing will reveal, but she cannot let herself be influenced by the excitement. She must treat it like any other sample, even though her hands shake like a novice as she breaks the seal of the envelope. She pushes the letter away. She is no state to read it. Instead she takes an old sample from a pile, squares up from the bottom and rules lines a quarter of an inch apart.

Her heart slows to meet the crisp 'shick' of her pencil on paper.

Shick, shick.

With each line she becomes steadier and more measured.

And not until each word has lost all meaning except the meaning inherent in its form does she reach again for the envelope and pull out January's letter.

The idea of January was born in the sea. On a cold grey day, the girl who I was walked fully clothed into the sea. It was a little death of sorts. The water stung her eyes and her limbs; the itch disappeared and with it her old life. When she emerged a few minutes later, she was light and nameless; she felt as if she had lost herself in the water, and it felt right.

The girl had spent her year trying to carve a niche for herself in the city. She had come to the city on the pretence of study, but really it was to find her place in the world. A place where she wasn't defined by her family, or her history. The trouble was, it wasn't that easy to shake off who she had been. It made matters worse that she had been simply playing at change; that her new life could be packed in a few boxes every university holiday, when she had to move out of halls.

Second year, she decided to become a true adult, and began to flat. She moved into a flat of boys who assumed that since she was a girl she'd cook and clean. The flat was dingily cheerful; traffic cones and stolen signs decorated the lounge and hallway. Hers was a little room. Her bed sat on a loft built by an industrious former flatmate, allowing room for a desk beneath. The view of the public walkway that ran past her window was obscured by a piece of badly dyed calico tacked to the wall above with push pins. She was loath to open it in case she pulled the whole thing down; the murky darkness suited her new lifestyle anyway. The flat was good enough if you didn't look too closely at the mould in the bathroom, the toilet that overflowed and the missing piles that had been replaced by a couple of two-by-fours bowed by the weight. She had noticed this once when she sat in the basement too stoned to move. Someone — no one was sure who — had moved a couch into the space, making it the perfect place for small gatherings. Especially if you could ignore the old needles from random junkies of times past. She had lost her virginity there, the scratch of the lumpy couch against her thighs and the musty smell of the dirt floor filling her senses. Thankfully her first lover was leaving for his OE soon after, so she didn't have to see him again. Even then she knew that there was no wisdom in screwing her flatmates. She was glad that her first time had not been marred by any romantic ideals like love. So immature, those ideas: adults know that sex is just sex.

It was all right, her new life; not a life that you would fantasise about, but she figured that you had to start somewhere. Halfway through the year her body began to rebel. Her skin began to itch and she began to resemble an open sore. The hippies at the health food store told her to cut out meat, dairy and wheat from her diet, and so she became a vegan by default. Her eczema cleared, but she began to crave meat. She became a self-righteous vegan then, not because of a deep-felt belief in animal rights but from simple jealousy. If she could not eat meat, then nobody should. She was plagued by chicken madness, spending afternoons watching them brown on the rotisserie at the supermarket, hoping that the aroma would satisfy her. One day, her resolve weakened and almost as if she was sleep-walking she found herself with a shopping bag filled with white bread, cheese and a beautiful glossy chicken. Her stomach cramped with each hasty bite: there is nothing as glorious as succulent chicken after a glut of chickpeas. The itch started almost immediately after the first bite, but she didn't care. It got worse and worse until it finally drove her into the sea.

'That's where I came in.'

January sounds as distant on the telephone as she had been in her story. It seems strange to Mae that this story rang more true, even though January's other letter had been more immediate and intimate. That's why Mae had to call her, to see if the girl was consistent; and she is: the almost clinical way January tells the story, as if she is looking at someone else, matches her disconnected writing.

'Don't you think it is strange, dear? You tell it like it happened to someone else; like you weren't there.'

'But that's the point, Mae. I wasn't there. That girl wasn't me; she doesn't exist any more.'

But who is the girl who replaced her, Mae wonders? A girl who lacks empathy and seems to want to keep the world at a distance; a girl who may never be able to learn the art as well as the science of graphology.

'I need to know more, January. I need to know the real you.'

'I've told you all I can.'

'It is not enough. I need you to be open; I need you to let down your guard so that I can teach you.'

'I don't think I can do that.'

Mae can hear the crack in January's voice, and hopes that it is the start she has been looking for. One more push and her wall will tumble down.

'Then I have nothing to teach you.'

Click.

Mae has pushed too hard, too soon.

seventeen

Mae wonders if the nurse's writing is as laboured as her speech; if her syllables stretch out across the page, taking forever to say one thing. Mae suspects it is for her benefit. Around others she bets the nurse is efficient and clipped.

'Do you understand what I'm saying, Miss Raine?'

'Mae, please.'

'Mae, you need around-the-clock care. Do you need me to organise somewhere for you?'

'I'll be fine at home.'

'Not by yourself. Do you understand me, Mae?'

Mae understands her perfectly well. She suspects that the nurse would like to send her off to practise dying with other people too old to matter any more.

No, that is not for Mae. If all goes according to plan, she'll be in front of her fire sipping tea by the end of the week. She just has a little Faustian deal to strike.

'We can arrange your care …'

'That won't be necessary. I just need to make a telephone call, dear.'

The nurse looks at January over her glasses, and January is suddenly aware that her coat has slipped off her shoulder. No, not slipped: she hadn't the time to pull her coat on properly since Mae's call; she just grabbed it and her bag and left the office. Alice had been good about it. All January said was, 'She's in the hospital. A ... friend,' and Alice had given her a taxi chit.

She tugs at the collar of the coat, making the snarl worse under the strap of her bag.

'Are you Miss Raine's caregiver?'

Something about nurses makes January feel as if she is a small child who has put a stolen gobstopper in her mouth under the very nose of the shopkeeper. Guilty and apologetic.

'Mae called me ...'

'This is for you.'

January expects a note from Mae, begging her to get her out of here, but it is a simple table of names and numbers.

'Some contacts, in case you need someone to cover for you. There will be times when you'll just need to get out of there, recharge your batteries. Caring for someone else can be draining.'

January folds the paper in on itself several times before shoving it deep into her bag.

'Go through and see her if you like, she's up for visitors.'

January had hoped for swinging doors that she could burst through, or at the very least curtains that she could sweep aside dramatically, the curtain hooks screeching against the rail. Instead there was a sliding door, its sound seemingly cushioned by the pervading gentle silence of the ward. Even January's voice is not immune to it: she impotently whispers, although she feels like yelling.

'Why does the nurse think I'm going to be taking care of you?'

'Thank you for enquiring, January. They're going to keep me in for a few days' observation, then I should get back to the cottage ...'

'They're letting you stay by yourself?'

'No, of course not. I will need help; your help.'

'Don't you think a nurse would be better ... I can't take care of you.'

'I'm not asking you to look after me. I'm offering you the chance to take care of yourself.'

'What are you offering, Mae?'

'I presume you still want to learn? I'll teach you. You will have access to all of my work my texts. All I need is your company until I get better. After that you can decide if you want to stay. The upstairs room would be yours, rent-free.'

'Why?'

Mae sighs as she shifts in the bed. 'Have you read about the man who made it to one hundred because he worked at the family bicycle shop every day since he was sixteen? Have you seen those people, suddenly old because they have nothing to get up for in the morning? I don't want that, January. I'm not prepared to retire from my life.'

January lets out her breath in a rush, as if for a moment she had forgotten how to breathe. 'Have you heard, January, of the law of inertia?'

A body in motion stays in motion.

The thought turns January's stomach, and the ground feels suddenly unstable.

'I ... need to go.'

She runs; runs out of the hospital grounds, runs away from the thoughts that addle her mind. It is finally a sharp stab of the stitch that halts her, doubled over and scrabbling for air. She slows her pace but keeps moving, dawdling aimlessly towards the water. If you walk without thinking in this city you always end up at the waterfront. The streets naturally pour toward the harbour like the rivers they replaced. January wonders if it is too early for a beer, and decides that if a pub is open then it must be all right. Sipping a beer and looking at the sea makes the world right again, although she is soon chilled to the bone by the prevailing wind. The sea always makes her feel better. She has read something about negative ions in sea breezes, and puts it down to that.

Good lord January. May as well paint yourself orange and call yourself Robert…

Inertia. Robert-the-quack's diagnosis still haunts her. She has moved physically but …

She gulps down the rest of her beer. Her body has the urge to move again, as if she can outrun her thoughts.

… But not emotionally. If she believed the self-help trash Alice was fond of she would probably take Mae's illness as a sign. She needs to move emotionally, and the universe has provided for her.

The cottage seems smaller without Mae. January sits at the kitchen table sipping tea from one of the small, fragile cups Mae prefers. Cat scoffs the food January has given her, making a disturbing purring crunching sound: probably the last sound you'd hear if a man-eating lion bore down on you. The thought of death sickens January. She moves out of the kitchen away from the reminder of Mae.

This whole place is a bloody reminder. Why did I come here?

She hadn't been able to resist the urge to look at the cottage. She looks at it now with an eye to carving out a place for herself; a new colour on the walls, her settee by the window and her rug finally unfurled on a floor. She can't help but imagine herself eating breakfast from her plates at the kitchen table.

Would it be worth it?

She ventures upstairs and opens the door to the spare room.

More junk, but it is far bigger than the room she lives in now. She moves the old trunks out and surveys the space.

I could live here.

As she sets to work cleaning out the room, that thought drowns out her nagging doubt.

Mae has been left dangling by that little shrew January. For sixty hours, fifteen minutes and forty-two seconds, give or take, she has been in delicious limbo. The anticipation made her feel like a teenager again, her stomach in knots as she waited and waited ... she must have skewed the nurses' observations terribly with her racing heart and fitful appetite. Mae wonders if Cassandra felt like this as she awaited the sack of her home, wishing her prophecy was wrong but knowing that she would be vindicated. It must have been a strange mix of triumph and despair when it finally happened: a mix not palatable to most people.

Much has changed in the few days she has been away. The floors have been cleared of paper; insurance, January says, against another fall. Mae hadn't expected January's invasion to be so thorough and quick. Already the cottage feels different; even smells different – a faint scent of roses, but there is no sign of flowers. Cat jumps on Mae's lap and they huddle together as if they are refugees hiding from the future that is happening around them.

I have become a teacher once more.

Mae sits in her chair sipping a cup of tea, just as she had predicted.

January has surprised me in the length of time it took her to decide. She has a penchant for the over-dramatic; it is not as if I asked for her soul, sealed with her name in blood. Well, not yet, anyway. Soon she will begin her studies in earnest.

It is relatively easy to come across as a caring person even if your heart is not in it: it all depends on the angle you take on the story. Leaving her flat had been easy: she simply made it seem as if it was all her flatmate's idea. He came across as a hero to his girlfriend and he even gave January her part of the bond and a couple of week's rent for the inconvenience. Grateful for her 'sacrifice', the girlfriend made him help January move, cramming her things into his car. January managed to thank him graciously despite his rough handling, and they even played at being friends, making fraudulent promises about keeping in touch.

The nurses, too, had treated her with a little more respect after she had told them that she would be caring for Mae. It could have been some kind of misplaced camaraderie; they had, after all, had to deal with Mae for the past couple of days. Maybe she would be known as Saint January in the ward now: a caregiver martyred by Mae.

Mae has been suspiciously quiet since they arrived back. It had been awkward for both of them, January unsure of how much support to offer and Mae unsure of how much to take. Hopefully, it will iron itself out. Of course if the roles were reversed, January would be a grumpy, stubborn thing too; it seems like one of the worst things that could happen to a person, the loss of independence. Especially to a woman who has obviously fended for herself for most of her life.

Mae seems to have nodded off in her chair, with Cat warming her lap. January wonders if she should wake her and move her to the bedroom, but decides against it. At least here she'll be warm in the sun; her bedroom is probably stone cold.

She gingerly lifts a box from the lounge floor. She only has a few left to unpack, and then she will have completely moved in. She tries to creep up the stairs silently, but each step creaks under her.

Better to do it quickly, like a sticky plaster.

She hopes she doesn't wake Mae as she takes a couple of steps at a time.

Tonight January will sleep in her own bed in her new room. Thankfully it hadn't rained this morning when the movers arrived with it, only an hour late. She has no idea how Mae can sleep on that mattress of hers; January felt as if it was sucking her in like quicksand. Perhaps that is why old ladies develop humps: years of sleeping on a mattress past its use-by date, claiming that it has some life in it yet.

She can't wait to get her linen on her bed. She loves the feel of the crisp cotton as she smoothes the sheets, and the perfection of a well-executed hospital corner. The box smells faintly of roses as she opens it. She is horrified when her hand emerges from the box covered in red ink. Her perfect, Egyptian cotton sateen, each of the 300 threads per square inch soaked in red. Red: like a scene from a B-grade splatter. Red: like the remains of a wedding night in the distant past. The mix of the colour and the cloying sweet scent of roses makes January think of the deflowering of a saint – sacred hymen blood staining the pure white cotton, hands that would usually be clasped in prayer twisting the sheet underneath as the pleasure in the pain becomes too much to bear. If her very expensive sheets hadn't been ruined that image alone would have made her laugh.

She immerses the sheet into a bath tub filled with cold water, pushing down the air-filled billows of cotton. Perhaps it won't be as bad as she thinks: the water has already turned pink.

She doesn't want to wake Mae, but she cannot leave her in her chair all night. By morning her legs would have seized up, and any progress they have made on the being-civil-to-one-another front today will be lost to crotchetiness. The preserve of the old and the self-righteous.

Mae looks younger in her sleep: more like the Mae January imagines reading her journal. Mae, her eyes hooded by Garbo lids so heavy that she looks through the long lashes that brush against her cheek, pouts in her lover's arms. He kisses her neck as she pulls her head away, letting it hang like it is broken. The light hits against her cheekbones, angling her into a femme fatale. January imagines Mae's life in high contrast and jarring angles, old film noir her only point of reference. Mae the lover. Mae the spy.

Mae the pain. Mae the grouch.

Mae turns out to be more like Garbo than January had thought, insisting that January bugger off and leave her alone.

It takes a fair amount of cajoling and pleading and finally a little force to get her out of the chair and into her room. Mae, channelling her inner adolescent, closes the door with a defiant slam.

January climbs into her bed. Free rent may not be worth it: Mae isn't living up to the character in her journal. Damn reality. People ought to behave how she imagines them.

In January's dreams that night, Mae is one of those open-mouthed clowns at a fun fair. January desperately tries to feed her with a spoon, but the turn of Mae's head is too quick. The food dribbles down her chin as her dull eyes turn left and right. January scrambles under the bright skirt of the stall, looking for the plug. Her knees are scraped and dirty but she crawls on. She finds it, and her hand hesitates. She closes her eyes and the horrific mask of Mae with her hollow eyes fills her with terror. She pulls so hard that after the Mae automaton turns off, the fair does too, and then everything else. January is left alone in the darkness.

She awakes, and pulls Cat beneath the covers. She lies awake listening to her soft breath, feeling her little heartbeat beneath her hand.

In the morning she awakes with her own hand against her chest, and for a moment is panicked that she can't feel anything. No reassuring thump of mortality. If she was really dead, the alarm would not be screeching at her to wake up, although January is not sure; only a corpse could manage to sleep through that alarm for a full ten minutes. She silences the alarm with a thud, and is blinded for a second by the low glare of the blue numbers. She lies staring at them until her eyes adjust.

7.30. 7.30? Somewhere along the way she has lost half an hour. She cannot even remember hitting snooze once, let alone three times.

She rushes around her room looking for something to wear in the pile of clothes stacked on her dresser. It seems more efficient this way, digging through the clothes she was too tired to put away: everything is at her fingertips. She finds a skirt and pulls it free, liberating its brethren to the floor. She'll just have to tidy them when she gets home from work.

Work. She's going to be late again. She hauls herself into the shower and counts Mississippi over and over in her head, accounting for every second.

The kitchen is quiet. She fills the kettle up and the sink is somehow reflected in the sky – dull and over-scoured. What excuse will she give Alice today? She could go with the truth and risk a lecture, or worse: helpful advice – *always set your clocks ten minutes ahead, then you'll never be late.*

She stirs milk into the tea, making it murky and sweet. She could tell Alice that she underestimated how long it would take to get to work, or that she twisted her ankle, or that she stopped to help an old lady ...

The quiet of the kitchen strikes her. Mae's teapot and cup are clean and cold to the touch. She should probably be sitting at the kitchen table by now, on to her second cup and tut-tutting about how half of the day is already gone. What if …

Her thought is cut off as she runs to Mae's door.

'Mae? Are you all right in there?'

Oversleep by five minutes and the whole place is on red alert. Mae listens to the handle on the door click several times before she opens her eyes for good.

Thump, thump: January's hand against the door.

'Mae? Are you awake?'

'Well, of course I am. Now.'

'Are you all right? Can you open the door?'

'I'm fine where I am, thank you.'

'Mae, you have to let me help you. I'll ring the nurse.'

'You wouldn't dare.'

'Are you coming out?'

'No.'

'Fine.'

There isn't time for this, this morning. Bloody stubborn old … January has tried to be understanding, tried to be patient, but this is wearing thin, fast.

She grabs a piece of paper and a long thin stick and tip-toes to the door.

That girl must wear lead in her shoes, the way she clomps around the house. Mae can hear her journey to the kitchen and back again without having to press her ear against the door. She's outside the door now, but she hasn't knocked …

The crafty little minx! As soon as the paper slips under the door, Mae knows what January is up to. The key slips out of the lock and into Mae's hand, and she drops it near the paper so January thinks she has her mark; the paper slips back under the door.

The paper is empty, but January is sure she heard the key drop. She peers through the keyhole, and falls back in horror as her gaze is returned by Mae's own eye. She rubs the back of her head, which took the full brunt of her surprise on the cupboard door.

'I still have the key.'

'You can't go locking yourself in your room. What if there was a fire?'

'Then I'd unlock the door.'

January sits against the door; she can hear Mae shuffling behind it. She straightens her back until she is at eye-level with the lock and twists around to peer into it. The key has been replaced: game on. She sinks back down against the door. Time to toy with Mae, just a little.

'If you don't come out, then I'm popping the hinges. Come to think of it, that's not a bad idea. Maybe I'll pop the hinges and confiscate your door.'

'You can't do that.'

'Can't I? I'm from the girls-can-do-anything generation. I own a drill.'

The lock turns and the door opens so quickly that January ends up flat on her back, grinning up at Mae.

'I don't know what you're smiling about. Go make yourself useful and make me a cup of tea.'

eighteen

'Start by sorting these.'

January is the miller's daughter, punished for her father's boasting with a room full of straw. Or in this case paper. Every apprentice must pay their dues: even Mae had begun by sorting samples for her mentor. She starts with the samples piled around the living room, seemingly making more piles rather than decreasing them. She sorts until the shapes blur and her fingertips are dry and then hauls herself upstairs, pins and needles stinging each step, to her bed. When she comes home from work the next day, she begins again Her exhaustion confuses her: at one point she is halfway through a pile when she realises that she has already sorted it.

Over three nights not a ring, nor a necklace, nor the promise of her first-born is exchanged, but it is her dearly held wish that some goblin would show up; at the very least to break the monotony. When she finally falls to her bed on the third night, every sample in the house has been sorted and filed, ready for her majesty Queen Mae's inspection.

'The best way to learn,' Mae says as she dumps a pile of samples on January's lap, 'is to do.'

She hands January a stack of plain paper and a fountain pen.

'The best samples are those on unruled paper and in fountain pen. Of course these days we have to make do with ballpoint, but fountain is easier for the beginner; you can see the pressure the person used in the writing itself. Ballpoint you can feel with the tip of your finger like Braille.' January looks wide-eyed and overawed. 'But we'll come to that later.'

January copies letters one by one from the originals to her blank page, like a naughty school girl writing lines over and over in a teacher's vain hope that morality would seep into the skin via chalk dust.

'You must copy each letter exactly. How does it feel to write like that? How hard do you have to hold your pen? How slowly is it moving across the page? How does your body feel physically when you form a letter?'

Night after night January copies. The letters have become just shapes; they no longer make sense.

She is not learning anything. Words go in and she regurgitates them out.

She looks at her hands, as if to check whether some actual lesson has seeped into her skin; nothing, except for the ink splotches on her fingers and a little dry skin between them. She scratches the dry spot. Perhaps the ink is seeping into her, the letters and the writing leeching into her brain like onomatopoeia. Or is that osmosis? She can't remember. No, nothing has changed. It's just an ink spot.

The blue ink splotch on her fingers is now a permanent mark, like she has been branded by her work. She is Mae's now, and no one can rustle her.

'Now,' Mae holds one of the transcripts in her hands, 'What can you tell me about the writer?'

'How am I supposed to know? You haven't taught me how to do that.'

'Haven't I? How did it feel to write it? How were you holding your pen?'

'Loosely.'

'How did that affect the pressure?'

'It was light, almost invisible.'

'The slope?'

'It kind of trailed off down the page, like the person didn't care by the time they reached the end of the page.'

'So can you tell me about the writer now?'

'They don't really care about what happens to them. They want to be invisible, unseen.'

'What kind of person do you think that would be?'

'I don't know. Depressed?'

'Good. You're getting there. It's like pulling teeth at the moment, but you're getting the gist of it.'

'Couldn't you have just told me that? What was the point in wasting all this time?'

'I could have told you. Or you could have looked it up,' Mae throws a large volume on graphology to January, 'but any parlour trick graphologist can do that. A master knows that the art is intuitive. A real graphologist will feel the pen in her hands as she reads a sample; will feel the tension in the writer's forearm and shoulders. Will know that the pressure on the page screams "look at me" or "please ignore me".'

'But this way is so slow. It's not like we have all the time in the world. You might drop dead any second.'

There is nothing like a well-timed reminder of your mortality to stop you dead in your tracks, so to speak.

There are times when Mae wishes January was a little more aware of social mores: that she was more like the pencil she uses to rule lines; that is to say, not so blunt. But then, Mae supposes, she'd be sharp, so it would be much of a muchness really.

Mae leans heavily against the desk and rubs her eyes.

'I think we should call it a night.'

'But we've hardly covered anything, Mae.'

'Are you determined to finish me off tonight?'

January helps Mae to her chair and pretends not to notice the pain Mae is trying to hide, instead silently slipping a couple of painkillers into Mae's hand.

Sometimes she gets it so right, and other times …

January's care is as inconsistent as her handwriting; she 'helps' with the things that Mae needs no assistance with, while neglecting the important things. Like tea.

As time passes she doesn't seem to be able to read Mae's moods. Some nights Mae will have more stamina than January, working well into the morning. Tonight is not one of those nights.

January is surprised how meditative this work can be. Her hands have settled into a steady tempo: sample, sharpen, square, rule. The words begin to lose their meaning and become abstract shapes: curves and lines, squiggles and dots. It is as if she can understand what is written without reading. She is well into the pile when she notices Mae sleeping soundly on her chair. It is then she notices the ache in her back, and as she twists to release it she can feel a ripple down her spine like her fingernail tracing the millimetre increments on the ruler in her hand.

January is slumped over her desk. Alice has brought her a cup of coffee, but she barely has the energy to sip it.

'Burning the candle at both ends?'

January cannot make sense of Alice's words. 'What?'

'Tired?'

'I'll be fine,' January drinks her coffee, 'after this.'

'Why are you so tired? Have you got a second job?'

'Something like that.'

'Well, I hope it's worth it.'

To tell the truth, January is not convinced that it is.

'You should give up your job and study full time,' Mae had said last night or a week ago. January is not sure.

'I can't, I don't have savings. How would I eat?'

'You're barely eating as it is.'

January had pinched her fingers around her wrist; each digit except for her little finger met her thumb. She has lost some weight, but she has a little while yet before she becomes A3.

She fills her nights studying old samples, religiously transcribing them like the monks of the middle ages. Each night she turns her hand to a new quirk of human nature; she knows how a person intent on murder would hold their pen, the pressure of first love. She copies other people's writing so much she can hardly remember what her own writing looks like. The traits of others have infected her, taken her over. It started with the ink spot on her finger. She had tried to protect her hands from infection by scrubbing them in hot, soapy water. The ink mark had faded a little, but refused to budge. It was as though her immune system had reacted to the invasion of foreign thoughts and behaviours leeching into her, cracking open and weeping. Mae had said that it was just the paper drying her skin, but January could feel that it was more; she could feel the pain of her swollen skin and the heat of her palms. The barrier cream she tried ruined the samples, and finally Mae ordered her to bring down an old trunk from upstairs. Mae's old kid gloves fit January perfectly.

She looks at her hands encased in their gloves. For a moment they look like they don't belong to her; someone else's hand has been clicked into her wrists, like she is a mannequin. She no longer has any control over her hands; she is merely a conduit for other people's thoughts and feelings.

Mae is energetic tonight. 'Now the real work begins.'

nineteen

'I've finished copying this pile Mae, what's next?'

Mae pushes herself up out of her chair and crosses to the bookcase. She runs her fingers over the books as if she knows them so intimately that she can distinguish them by touch. She gives January a book and settles down into her chair once more.

'Read this.'

'I thought the best way to learn was to do.'

'Then copy the examples in the book – just give me a little peace girl.'

Mae is fading. Her skin is becoming more and more transparent, and the contrast between it and the inky blue of her veins is becoming more pronounced. Soon she'll be as insubstantial as the company she keeps. January is oblivious to them, but Mae can hear the ghosts that they've conjured scratching at her door and whispering through cracks, their pleas for attention keeping her awake at night. It is worse than Mae has ever experienced before. Perhaps the quacks at the hospital were right: perhaps she should be resting. But she can't rest here; January's hunger for knowledge is as demanding as the ghosts' desire for existence. January's enthusiasm sustains them. Mae shudders to think of them feeding off her – the dark circles under January's eyes evidence of her life being drained away.

It is settled. Time apart would be good for both of them. Mae's things are packed into her small suitcase well before the dawn light reflects off the first passenger carriage.

January insists that Mae take a taxi to the train station.

'It's not very far, I can walk.'

'You're the one who wants a few days' rest. I won't have you collapsing on the way to the station.'

The way Mae had fussed that morning made January glad for a few days off. She had woken to Mae already packed and waiting to leave. Anxious to be leaving January in charge of Cat, she had spent last night going over what should be done in her absence – as if January was a stranger who had never lived here. In the morning she went over it again, talking at the bathroom door while January showered and dressed.

'Don't overfeed Cat.' Mae hands January a small card inscribed with equally small writing. 'The number where I can be reached …'

January shoves the card in her pocket and Mae out the door. 'Mae, the taxi is here …'

'I don't need a taxi, I can walk.'

January rides in the taxi with Mae to the station to make sure she doesn't get out once the cottage disappears around the block.

'There's no need to worry. I did a great job last time you were away.'

Mae tries to disguise her smile with a frown, her mouth as lopsided as a right-hander's attempt at writing with their left.

'It'll be fine. Cat will be fine, and I'll keep busy with your lessons.'

'You should take time off too, visit your friends.'

The awkward silence in the taxi lasts until they reach the station. January offers her hand and is pulled into a hug which is rigid and all angles.

'I'll see you in a couple of days, Mae.'

'Take care of everything, January, including yourself.'

January starts the short walk to the office, tucking the card Mae gave her into her journal for safe keeping. She feels lighter, as if her feet are no longer anchored to the ground. A few days making believe that the cottage is hers, in which to move furniture and plan colour schemes. She hums to herself as she walks to her desk, suddenly realising that the office seems to be deserted. Has she come in on a Saturday? She flicks on her computer to check her calendar, and sees a note taped to her monitor.

You're late. Go to the staff room. Alice ☺

The whole world seems to be in slow motion. Ted's lips move open and shut like a goldfish gasping for air. The staffroom is overcrowded: designed for a few bodies at a time and not the entire floor. Alice is up the front with Ted: this impromptu meeting is being held in her honour. Alice blushes a beetroot red: it spreads across her face and chest like a stain on a tablecloth.

Alice has got the job.

Her desk has already been cleared, her nick-nacks sitting in a box in Ted's office. The desk seems smaller without her, in some kind of backwards way: usually things seem bigger when something is missing, but it was as if Alice's cubicle had swelled to accommodate her. The only evidence that she has even been here is the coffee ring groove where Chairman Meow used to sit.

January looks up to see a sullen A1 staring at her. She looks as if she has just been broken to bridle: out of breath and uncertain of her own volition.

'Alice would like to see you in her office.'

January waves her hand towards A1 like it is some sort of magic talisman.

'I'm busy.'

A1 snorts and turns away so fast that January is frightened that she'll throw a shoe.

'Like I care what you do. But I'm telling Ted …'

A1 stops, as if she needs such a massive amount of brain power to process her thoughts that all other functions must cease. She shakes her head and slowly starts up again, like a carousel horse lurching to life.

'Alice just wants to see you, OK?'

It must be something about that office, because Alice pops her head out of the door at the sound of her name like Ted always did. It reminds January of the game at the arcade where little plastic animals pop up randomly and you have to hit them on the head. Alice beckons January with a couple of fingers. She looks as if she is trying to be friendly, but the effect is patronising; it sets January's teeth on edge. What she wouldn't do for a foam-covered hammer right now.

Her feet feel sluggish as she walks across the office floor. It is like a scene in a movie where the camera zooms out and the protagonist's walk seems to stretch for miles. Alice is now her manager: in control of her life for most of her waking day. She can't even bullshit Alice as she did Ted: after four years of being that close, Alice knows all her habits. January suspects that this is what this 'little talk' will be about: Alice warning her, telling her that she'll be keeping an eye on her. January can foresee a miserable future of actual work ahead of her. She's not sure if she can work for Alice. How can she take any orders from Alice seriously, when she knows what she is like? Their 'friendship' will necessitate Alice making an example of January, so she can assert her power. It will be some great show so the rest of the plebeians will whisper in horror among themselves: *If she could do that to her friend, what will she do to us?*

January wonders if her job description will be changed to reflect her new role: scapegoat, whipping boy, long-suffering Job?

The office is a strange Ted/Alice hybrid, her things half out of a box and his half in. Chairman Meow sits awkwardly on his new desk, eyeing the framed photos of Ted's family suspiciously. Ted, it seems, has made himself scarce. This makes January even more nervous: flaying rarely happens in public these days. January imagines her head atop a pike, staring blankly at her co-workers. Just another day at the office: they're probably used to her lifeless eyes already.

Alice pauses, swinging back on her chair a little, which makes January worried that she'll topple out the window behind her.

'I've thought about you for a long time, January. You're not really happy in your job, are you?'

January is unsure what to say. The truth is that she *is* unhappy about her job; she always has been. But that's not something you want to say to your boss. She tries a non-committal diagonal nod: neither up and down nor a shake of the head.

'So I thought you might enjoy a new challenge, where we'd work closely together. I thought you'd like to be my assistant.'

'Assistant manager?'

'Well, no. *My* assistant.'

January imagines herself losing half her body weight and joining the stables at reception.

'We could still hang out with each other every day. The feng shui expert said the best corner for you to sit in would be over here.'

January imagines the Situations Vacant ad for her position.

Are you an unmotivated no-getter who is sick of a challenge? Do you suffer fools gladly? Do you have limited aspirations for your future? If you answered 'yes' you're the perfect fit for our company. Welcome!

Maybe working for Alice wouldn't be too bad.

'What would I have to do?'

There had been a definite perverse twinkle in Alice's eye when she sent January out to get her a coffee. Now that she's in the big leagues Alice is no longer satisfied with the coffee-flavoured granules that the rest of the office drinks with a grimace: she wants coffee that tastes of coffee. January screws the ten-dollar note in her hand into a little ball as she waits in line. It seems that her whole life has been like this: waiting for something for someone else.

She lifts her gaze to the mirrors behind the counter and sees him walking into the cafe. She doesn't believe the mirror, and turns; he is standing right behind her, only inches away.

He looks straight past her as if he doesn't recognise her at all, and for a moment January doubts if he would: she can't recall if he has ever looked at her face intently. Perhaps the bright light of day has confused him; she is a woman of twilight and shadows to him. She gasps a little too loudly when she sees the fall of black hair and the bright smile behind him.

Olivia. He cannot acknowledge January because of Olivia. O-Liv-I-A. Each syllable would roll off January's tongue covered in her bitterness, spat out on the ground like venom sucked from a wound. If January dared to say it.

'Miss?' The barista waits for her order.

'Uh, two flat whites to go.'

She waits at the counter for her coffee and watches them in the mirror as they order.

'A long black for me, and ... Livvy? What would you like?'

'Green tea.'

'And a green tea.'

He puts his arm around Olivia and kisses her forehead. January can't believe he did that right in front of her. She grabs the coffee in two hands and heads for the door, but struggles to open it.

Suddenly he is beside her, opening the door. 'Here, let me help you.'

January stammers a thank you, confused by his attention.

'No problem,' he winks. 'I love a damsel in distress.'

She is outside, and can breathe again. The outside tables are abandoned: it is too cold today to people-watch. She wishes she hadn't 'given up' smoking; then she'd have an excuse to sit outside in the cold. She watches as he and Olivia take a seat by one of the large windows of the cafe. She should go, just walk back to the office, but she sits at the small table that mirrors the couple's table inside.

She is on the same side as Olivia, and but for the pane of glass that separates them, she could be enjoying her coffee with him. Each smile and shared joke is for her, not Olivia, and when he leans over the table to kiss his wife, January can feel it on her own lips. She opens her eyes to see them both staring at her. January picks up her coffee and leaves.

'This is cold.' Alice wrinkles her nose.

'It was busy.'

'We should get a plunger then. Would you look into that for me, Jan? Thank you.'

Alice dismisses January with a wave of her hand and goes back to arranging her desk.

'Whiptchhhh ...' Al mimes cracking a bullwhip as January walks past. She decides to ignore it.

I'm nobody's bitch.

But at her desk she begins to doubt her conviction. He has all the power, choosing when she exists to him.

An email from Alice: January jabs 'delete'.

How could he do that to her? Ignore her and then pretend to be a gallant gentleman, holding the door open for her?

Her phone rings, and she ignores it.

I love a damsel in distress. Is that why he did it?

The phone rings again and January picks it up. 'Yes?'

'Alice wants to see you,' A1's voice is light with laughter. 'And by the way? Whiptchhhh …'

At five, January heads out the door. Alice pops her head out of her office. 'Jan?'

What now? But through her teeth January says, 'Yes?'

'I thought we could go out for a drink, to celebrate?'

'I have plans.'

'Oh. Maybe tomorrow?'

'Maybe.'

She has been stewing on it all day: the way he treated her – no, the way he *treats* her. She had decided around lunchtime that she would confront him, and spent a good portion of the day imagining the look on Olivia's face when she told her the truth. The heat of her resolve makes the walk down the Terrace and up Bolton Street shorter than expected. There are still a few people in the gardens as she walks to her tree and waits.

She rubs her neck and the ache travels up to her temples, helped along by the chatter of the birds around her preparing to roost.

And so too her lovebirds. The headlights of their car make January squint, and she can only make out their silhouettes as they climb up the stairs. Olivia is laughing, and pauses to kiss him. It is a long kiss: the kind that is a promise of more to come. Olivia takes his hand and they run up the rest of the stairs.

She waits until they are at their door before she crosses the road and begins her ascent. She takes a deep breath and looks up. This is the closest she's ever been to the yellow house, and for a moment she is more excited to be here than scared. As she climbs, dread replaces her butterflies. Tonight she takes control, no matter what he says.

The door is a bright, shiny red, with a brass lion-head knocker. She is about to knock when she notices the door is slightly ajar. She nudges it and it opens; in the hallway are Olivia's high heels and his coat. They were too eager to get upstairs to bother to lock the door.

January is grateful Mae had insisted she wear the gloves. The fine leather stretched over her hands makes her think of them as someone else's hands, which she has no control over. It pleases her to think that she can leave no trace of herself, that she has become a shadow. She likes to think of herself as a sentence constructed by a pen that barely touched the paper: a ghost in ink. It makes her feel sure, this artifice, that she is doing nothing wrong. A home cannot be invaded by a ghost, only haunted. Not that January thinks of this as an invasion: she feels entitled to be here. She takes her time to run her hands over their things, imagining that this is her home. Her vase, her chair, her smile on her wedding day. January leaves the frame face down, suddenly feeling like she has been caught out; like she is being watched.

The rash on her arm has cleared, but the habit of the itch remains. She rubs her arm with her gloved hand. It is a strange sensation, like someone else is touching her. She decides to heighten the illusion by wrapping herself in his coat, picked up from the floor. The smell and scratch of it is suddenly arousing. It is like she has been trained to react in this way: a Pavlovian dog salivating at the sound of a bell. She lies on their couch, closes her eyes and touches herself with the tenderness with which he touches Olivia: a soft caress of the cheek that trails down her throat to trace the round of her breast. She imagines Olivia, stripped of clothes, gently unhooking her earrings, looking more beautiful free of adornment. For a moment she is confused by her senses: she can no longer tell if it feels like another hand is touching her or like her hands are touching Olivia's body. In this moment January can only see Olivia: her face and hair. She cannot recall his face or even her own; her memory is blotted out by the beauty of Olivia's lips stretched into an 'o' of pleasure. Her legs ache from tension, and her body is wracked by cramps. She waits a while until her breath returns to normal before she climbs the stairs.

She can't believe that she is this close to them. So vulnerable in their sleep: he instinctively puts an arm around Olivia and pulls her closer to his body. To January it feels as if he has punched her in the same spot: she feels winded and out of breath. She pulls the gloves off and shoves them deep into the pockets of his coat. Her hand hovers over Olivia's face. She wants to touch her skin; she wants to hold her hand over Olivia's mouth and see her eyes open in horror. Instead she covers her own mouth and kneels down beside the bed. She is so close to Olivia's face that she can feel her sweet sour breath against her cheek. January cocks her head so that she is eye to eye with Olivia, like her head rests on the same pillow. She stares at Olivia's face, trying to scry for her true personality. What it is that makes Olivia so beautiful?

The small smile on Olivia's face as his arm holds her tighter shocks January out of herself. She creeps out of their home, shaken at how close to insanity she has been walking. But she has gone to the edge and made it back alive and intact; she even has a souvenir to prove it. Now that she has his coat, she won't need to go to the house again.

The walk home seems new in this light. She is no longer recognised by the street, and the shadows threaten with a fearful symmetry. She has not until now seen the violence of the light: not letting any creature hide as it slices the night with its claws. She stops short of the street light: she doesn't need the reality of light just yet. In the shadows her actions are not quite real. Her hands are clean, metaphorically. But they are cold; they are unused to being naked. She blows on them; the steam of her breath hangs in the air. The gloves are cold, and sticky with hand cream. January shoves them back into her pocket and tucks her hands into her armpits. The sensitive skin tingles immediately; she closes her eyes and bites her lip. Something else is different tonight. It is eerily quiet. She smiles. Perhaps the bird finally realised the futility of its song and flew away.

It is like a blow to her stomach when she notices the small body on the concrete.

Bloody cats.

But the feathers are intact, the throat untorn. The bird in her hands is perfect, except that it is obviously dead. Exhausted perhaps by its perpetual song. January wants to give it a proper burial, sickened by the thought of its body being consumed by scavengers. It is not until after she has placed the bird in the grave and replaced the last handful of dirt that it occurs to her that the bird may have died of disease.

The dirt mingles with the ink stains on her fingers, threatening to seep into the cracks in her skin. This must be how diseases jump from one species to another – micro-organisms using empathy as a bridge. The tingle of the nerves in her fingers reacting to the cold night air feels like a colony of bacteria multiplying.

She tip-toes around the cottage, marvelling at how much noise a person can make when they are trying to be quiet, before she remembers that she is alone.

Alone.

She flicks on the bathroom light. She scrubs her hands obsessively, scrubbing away all traces of tonight, filling the basin with fresh water at least three times. She steps into a scalding hot shower, scrubbing her body with a nail brush as she has seen in the movies.

She lets the water run over her, her tears disguised by the larger drops of the shower. She is not sure why she is crying. Not for the loss of the bird; not even for the loss of him. Maybe she laments the lost years: the years when she had walked past this tiny cottage lost among the roots of a high-rise forest, not knowing her future waited. She must be over-tired to cry like this. Like the mother of a newborn she has been catching sleep when she can; in between work, tea-making and her lessons. The strange thing is that at times January feels as if she needs no sleep; often she works late into the night not noticing the hours pass by. This is the first thing she has ever fully committed herself to, and she loves it here.

Cat blinks as the light snaps on. She shoos Cat off the bed and out the door, closing it on the indignant tail sauntering down the stairs. Alone now in her room, she holds the coat to her chest, the wool prickling her already raw skin. Her body betrays her. The blood rushes to her lips, making them plump. She considers sleeping in the coat, but decides instead to sleep beside it, a pillow stuffed inside to give it some form.

Finally, a guy in my bed.

She snuggles into the coat, the fibres pickling her nerves, making her skin feel extra sensitive. She rolls her back into it, resting her head on an outstretched arm. Something is not quite right. She takes the other arm and wraps it around her, so that she is straitjacket tight in the coat's embrace. Safely cocooned within him, just like Olivia.

This is all she wants, and this is all she needs.

On the verge of sleep some time later, she almost believes it.

twenty

It is never this dark in the city. Here it is complete; it envelopes you. For a moment Mae fancies that she hasn't opened her eyes at all, so she closes them again to feel the weight of her eyelids. She holds the back of her hand in front of her face and slowly opens her eyes again, waiting for the familiar shape to emerge out of the dark. It takes a moment to see it, but like a true scientist she doesn't trust her first result.

She snaps on her bedside lamp, impatient for the arrival of the sun. Perhaps she could coax the embers in the wood range to life, and have the first cup of tea brewing to greet Cheryl this morning.

A chill has crept into the house between the cracks in the floorboards and the weatherboards. In a few hours the house will groan with life as the sun warms it, but now she tip-toes to the kitchen, every squeak of floorboard echoing in her ears. *She has me trained already.* Consideration for others is a hard habit to break, it would seem. Mae adheres to it even though she is alone; even though January is at least a couple of hours south of here.

Even though that girl could sleep through a train wreck undisturbed.

Perhaps it is a harder habit to form: Mae has seldom heard January soften her steps or, for that matter, her manner. And although she knows that January will not change, Mae has fallen into that trap of mothers and lovers – believing that she can change someone with a little guidance – and feels the disappointment of her error.

Mae sees potential in January, she is sure of it, but January lacks something. She is a diligent student and learns her lessons thoroughly, but she gets too caught up in the detail. There are times Mae can see the characteristics of a page plainly on January's face – a frown of frustration or a downcast lip of sadness. January is a sponge absorbing it all, but she doesn't retain anything. If Mae gave her one good squeeze she wouldn't be surprised if it all dribbled out. January doesn't have the finesse, the innate sense of the art.

She's not me …

It only takes a week for Mae to figure out what the real problem is. It has nothing to do with the student. The frustrations of explaining the patently obvious and the strange questions January would ask: Mae had blamed these on January's failure as a student, not on her own failings as a teacher.

She wanders down the hall to the sitting room with the lights off, feeling like a child again in her nightgown – her hands fluttering about helping her find her way in the dark. If a real child like Jasmine saw her now they'd probably think her a ghost.

The mean light in the sitting room does not take the chill off the air. Mae leaves the door open so that the warmth from the wood range in the kitchen has a chance to penetrate the cold air in the room. She pulls her dressing gown close around her and settles at her desk. A faded photograph of her family – ghosts trapped behind glass – watches over her shoulder. Mae takes her time sharpening her pencil and arranging the blank page of paper in front of her. She measures lines down the side, nicking the margin with her pencil at regular intervals. She squares out from the nick and rules firmly, *shick shick* down the page. Her mind clears as she focuses on the rhythm of her hand, her breath, her heart.

'You're up early today. Feeling better?'

A hot cup of tea sits beside the stack of papers that Mae has ruled. She picks up the cup and enjoys the crackle of pins and needles in her fingers.

'Much.'

Cheryl drops her gaze and shuffles her feet, suddenly the young awkward teenager Mae remembers from a decade ago.

'Do you feel up to company? You know I wouldn't normally ask, but …'

Mae pats Cheryl's hand. 'You don't need to ask. I'll look after the little monster.'

'It should only be for a couple of hours. I'll drop her off when the others go to school. She'll have her colouring things so she should be quiet …'

Mae sips her tea, staring at her pile of papers as the tannin spreads across her tongue.

'You're busy. I can find someone else. I shouldn't have asked …'

'Cheryl, I'd like to look after Jasmine. We'll have a great time.'

'Are you sure?'

'Go and organise her now, before you persuade me otherwise.'

The backpack strapped to Jasmine makes Mae feel more school ma'am then she is comfortable with. Even her greeting has been infected with the role, her 'Good Morning, how are you today?' delivered in that awful sing-song voice that swings too high at the end. Mae has prepared for the visit, spreading her ruled paper on the kitchen table and placing a few markers in a mug in a carefully planned casual way.

Jasmine doesn't seem to notice, climbing onto a chair and dumping the contents of her bag onto the table. A brightly coloured felt-tip rolls close to the edge of the table before Mae puts her hand on it with a snap that frightens both of them. Mae puts the marker into the mug.

The child is too absorbed by her own work to notice Mae. Mae is patient, filling pages with the same twenty-six letters, lower and upper case, in a large rounded hand. Fifty-two familiar forms march across the leaves: one for each week. But fifty-two weeks could never be enough to learn all the different manifestations of these simple letters.

'Mae, what are you doing?'

'I'm drawing, dear.'

Jasmine leans over the table so far she is almost lying on it.

'You're not drawing.'

'Yes I am.'

'Those are ABCs Mae. You can't draw those.'

'Then what am I doing?'

Jasmine has inherited her sigh from her mother. 'Writing. You write ABCs.'

'What are you doing then?'

Jasmine rolls her eyes and picks up her book. 'Drawing, Mae.'

'Not writing?'

'No, I'm too little to write.'

'Is that so?'

Jasmine pops the lid off her green marker, concentrating its tip in the pupil of the princess's eye. Mae's *hmm* disturbs her, and she looks up again.

'It's a little bit funny, you saying that you can't write. It seems to me that drawing and writing are the same.'

Jasmine looks at the marker in her hand and then at the marker in Mae's. She recognises the shapes Mae draws – circles and lines, shapes that she can draw herself.

Mae leans over the table and whispers in Jasmine's ear, 'I can show you how to write: all you need to do is copy me.'

Jasmine is a quick student; her smile mirrors Mae's.

She masters her letters quickly. After the first day she shrugs off Mae's guiding hand, preferring to trace over pencilled-in shapes.

Mae spends her last night at home with pencil in hand, creating practise sheets for Jasmine and a last gift – the alphabet sweeping across a poster two by two (hurrah, hurrah) in bold black strokes.

'This is for you, Jasmine.' Mae hands Jasmine the rolled-up poster, which she has tied with a ribbon.

'Oh Mae,' Cheryl hugs her. 'You didn't have to.'

'Well of course I didn't have to. I wanted to.'

'What do you say, Jasmine?'

'Thank you Mae.'

Mae bends down to Jasmine's level and takes a sweet out of her purse. 'This is for you too. Don't tell your mother.'

'Thanks Mae'. Jasmine gives Mae a sloppy kiss on the cheek.

'Now you take care of yourself, Mae.'

'No need, Cheryl. I have someone to do that for me.'

'You tell that January that if anything happens to you she'll have me to answer to.'

'Don't worry, Cheryl. I'm fine. I'll come back and see you soon.'

'You'd better.'

They continue to wave long after the train has pulled away.

The train ride home is prose written by a dullard: each minute is deliberate and laborious. Mae imagines the large, child-like circles the wheels scribe over and over again; a straight line of 'o's stretching from here to Wellington. She can imagine Jasmine practising them – with her tongue out and forehead furrowed, absorbed by the task.

Had Mae seen the same look on January's face? Although it is dangerous to think of her as a child – Mae can imagine the arguments that would ensue if she dared to use her school ma'am voice at home – January does need patience and a firmer guiding hand. Mae will provide it as long as January needs her.

She is surprised by January when she gets off the train. Not by her presence – Mae had expected an escort home since she had been dropped off here a week ago – but by the way January looks. She seems taller and almost radiant. Mae can't think what the difference is, until she realises that January is smiling.

'You look well. I guess you needed a few days to yourself.'

'I think you were right, Mae.'

January's life is now authored by a confident hand. Her days progress with a steady regularity: breakfast with Mae, walk to work, then home again and then lessons. The rash on her neck has cleared completely, although she still wears her gloves to protect her hands. Eventually she will shed these too, and her skin will emerge pale and baby soft.

Every day, on the way home, January clears the post office box. Every day she hopes for a little surprise: a new sample from a mailout addressed to her. Mostly the mail is for Mae; she has been sending out enquiries for many years.

One day, there it is, on a creamy white envelope: her name scratched in red. January knows it is from him, even though she has never seen his writing before today. It has the same roughness as their coupling – an edge of desperation. She imagines his lips forming each of the letters as they are written; the tongue-twister of a start followed by the purr of her last syllable. She closes her eyes and covers her mouth with three of her fingertips, her middle finger resting in the bow of her lips and the other two in the corners, her thumb and little finger resting under her jaw. She silently says her own name over and over, feeling the rise and fall of her lips, the movement of her jaw. Her name becomes a passionate kiss, and January almost loses herself in it before she is interrupted.

'Are you all right, Miss?'

She blushes as red as the ink on her letter. She thrusts the envelope deep in her bag, and seeks a more private place to open it. Their relationship has always been clandestine, and she sees no reason to change that now.

It must remain a secret, especially from Mae. She would be horrified if she read this: the erratic slope of emotional instability and the pent-up lettering so common in serial killers, controlled and calculated. His small, tight words hunch on the page as if they are waiting for their chance to pounce; the angular connections between the letters snarl at her and the ovals of the vowels are closed off like the narrowing of a predator's eye. Mae would say he was a psychopath and that January is not to see him; she would lock her up in her tower. January values Mae's opinions, and that is why she must never see this letter. January doesn't want the magic to end.

She knows what his writing says. She knows it is at odds with his words, but she also knows his passion; knows that her love would soothe him, change him.

January,

Tonight I will dream of you how you ought to be: majestic; a goddess among men.

I have missed you. Why do you hide from me? What have I done? What can I do to win you back?

Yesterday I thought I saw you. I followed your shadow through the streets, every nerve aching to be with you, to feel the familiar press of your body against mine. I touched her hair and I knew it was wrong: not your scent, not your gentle curl, not you, January.

Today I thought I heard your laugh and it thrilled me ...

She re-reads every line, committing each part to her memory. She tries to read just the words, banishing what his writing is saying.

The letters start to arrive every other day, and each time January's body is alive with adrenaline. She can't wait to rip the envelope open and devour every word, but she always restrains herself. Torturing herself with delicious anticipation, each minute of delay seems to stretch, and it feels as if she has lived a year. She allows herself the smallest respite during the walk home, holding the envelope, tracing her name with her finger so often that the paper is soft and furry. She'll let herself open a tiny corner of the seal, and breathe in the heady scent of roses, paper and desire. It carries her through the night, through each lesson that Mae teaches until January is finally alone in the dark of the night to open it. She feels as if she knows every line before she reads it: like his thoughts have seeped through the paper during the day and infiltrated her mind.

January lights a candle as reverently as if she was in church. Reading the letters has become a kind of prayer; the elaborate ritual a testimony to her faith. Like the faithful she prays for a life better than her own; a life that is too perfect to be on earth. A life she doesn't deserve. The letter itself has become almost redundant.

She reads until her eyes become heavy with exhaustion, then she climbs into bed, comforted by the closeness of his letters underneath it, directly under her heart. They have become a talisman; protecting her in her sleep.

Tonight I will dream of you.

twenty-one

A breeze tugs at the brim of Mae's hat, threatening to topple its perch. It is not the done thing these days, taking pride in your appearance, but Mae believes it shows respect for all those around you. A woman who doesn't try must be very conceited indeed; she must think that she cannot improve on herself.

What a marvellous day to be a grump with the world! Today Mae shall embrace the crotchety old woman that she is – well, that she's certainly justified in being, after this morning's performance.

January had been hopping around the cottage like a demented version of the White Rabbit.

I'm late! I'm late!

How January can sleep through the screech of her new alarm is beyond Mae.

Perhaps Mae might drop into a shop or two and pretend to be feeble-minded. It is always a pleasant amusement to watch shop assistants try to help her no matter how annoying and difficult she's being. It always fascinates her how far you can push them: they always come back for more, eager for a sale. The poor things – quite literally, she imagines, struggling on minimum wage and having to deal with people like Mae. For most of them it is probably their first job – imagine that baptism by fire. It is too easy to forget what it is like to be young and struggling against everything; not just money, but who you are and your place in the world. Or what the world expects of you.

Does she expect too much from January? She had known that the lessons and the living arrangement would be a challenge …

Since Mae returned January has been fading; bleached like she has been left in the sun. Her spine has curled back into a hunch, the dark circles have returned under her eyes and her smile had proved to be short lived.

Perhaps it's me. Mae's wry smile twists into a frown when she realises that it could be; but what can she do? It's not as if she can just leave town every few weeks – she simply cannot afford the time. No, they'll just have to work out a way that they can live together. Mae can alleviate some of the pressure on January by doing a bit more, especially now that she feels strong again. Though she cares not a jot for dusting, she can clear her own mail: a job she has missed. There is nothing like the thrill of finding a letter addressed to you and the anticipation of what secrets the envelope may contain. It had never felt like a chore to Mae, but January doesn't need to know that.

For a moment, Mae feels disorientated by the rows of bright red boxes. Everything is familiar but strange; things she did without thinking are now clear and distinct. The small pocket in her purse that holds the key, the number of steps from the door to her box, the number on the box – white carved out of black. The key feels too small in her hand, as if it has shrunk. Or perhaps she has grown? Mae shakes the White Rabbit thoughts from her head as she opens her mail box.

She notices a small white envelope addressed in red. The image of the red of the post box and the snow white of the envelope is so perfect it is almost a shame to disturb it. But disturb it she must.

It is not for Mae, but for January. The red of the ink makes it look as if her name has been cut into pale flesh. Just touching the envelope fills Mae with dread. She does not want to conjure this person who is plainly erratic and possibly dangerous – the large felon's claw from the 'y' that threatens the address below like a looming guillotine is proof enough. Better to take it home and deal with it there. The best thing for January is if Mae disposes of the letter before she sees it. Although even with her rudimentary knowledge, January would know the danger she was in immediately. Mae's fear hastens her journey home.

The embers are still warm, so lighting a fire is easy. Cat rubs herself against Mae's legs.

She hesitates before throwing the letter into the fire. She wants to examine the letter more closely. If she had received this as an answer to one of her cards ... but she hasn't received it. The letter is for January. But it is a hard habit to break, her curiosity of humanity, and while she reflects on this she realises that she has already broken the seal.

January,

Why have you not answered me?

Mae gasps and folds the letter again. This is not the first letter. January has been hiding this from Mae.

She knows January will hate her for doing this, but she doesn't care. She opens the door to January's room and is surprised by her own hesitation. She takes a breath and shakes her head. Privacy doesn't matter any more; this is for her own good.

She tries to forget the names she used to call her father when he looked through her things. She is not a snoop as she looks for more letters in January's drawers. She is not a sneak as she opens each of January's books, looking for secrets tucked in the leaves. Nothing.

The bed. Where Mae herself would hide her things when she was young; but would January be so … obvious? She lifts the bedspread. She can see an old tin heavy with letters. Did Pandora hesitate before she opened her jar? Mae pulls the lid from the tin. It is worse than Mae thought; from the postmarks these letters have arrived almost daily. She doesn't have to read them; their relationship is clear: dark, erratic and definitely sexual. What is most disturbing is how this man regards January; her name is dwarfed by the other letters, his flourish on the 'J' almost closing her in completely and the hook on the y threatening to scratch her out. He doesn't want the world to know about this 'relationship'. He probably has a wife. Mae needs to cut out this rot immediately.

'Mae? Are you home?'

January's arrival home is greeted by silence and darkness. She hesitates turning the light on, remembering the twist in her stomach when she had broken into the cottage. Perhaps this time her premonition will come true, perhaps Mae is lying on the floor …

Mae is not home. January has checked every room, with Cat following behind her. There are no appointments on the calendar; she can't even call Mae's cell phone, because Mae does not have one.

She makes herself a cup of tea; the only thing she can think to do. She sips it at the kitchen table, searching through the day's mail. At least one mystery is solved: the post box had been empty on her way home tonight. The event was so unexpected that January had checked the number on the front, in case somehow she had managed to open the wrong box; but it was correct, and it was empty: not even hope was clinging to the bottom.

There is no familiar white envelope for her today. She checks through the stack of mail again in case she missed it, but it is not there. Perhaps something happened last night so he couldn't send it: perhaps it was put in the wrong post box and will be delivered tomorrow, or perhaps it has disappeared to the same place as Mae. January raises the tea to her lips, but when the cold liquid hits her tongue she spits it back into her mug. The world has become icy; she hugs her arms around her as she walks to the sitting room to build a fire. Cat is already in front of the dying embers, her fur puffed up to trap the last of the warm air. The fire takes little coaxing to revive itself, January feeding it with newspapers and kindling before placing a couple of good logs on top. Cat is left to guard the flames as January climbs upstairs, eager to be out of her work clothes. She peels them off, smarting at the chill that numbs her skin. She turns on the shower, wanting a quick blast of heat on her limbs. As she showers she remembers the times in her old life when she would stand under the water until it ran cold. Her reflection is blurred with steam; she is a ghost of herself as she smoothes on moisturiser. She pulls on the comfortable clothes she thinks of as her uniform. Her gloves usually complete it, but tonight they have slipped into the sink, and water has seeped into the fingers. January tosses them into the washing basket and does not stop for another pair; she is eager to be in front of the fire. It will do her skin some good to be able to breathe.

'Mae?'

There is still no answer. Perhaps Mae has gone to a movie, or is visiting friends; although January doesn't know if she has any – not that she's ever asked. Perhaps she's gone to the house up north for a while; but surely she would have said something.

'She wouldn't just leave us, eh Cat?'

January pulls a quilt around her and settles in the chair to wait. Cat jumps on her lap, and January folds her in the quilt as well. Her worry is soon outweighed by the warmth of the room and the rhythm of Cat's breathing, and the late nights claim their due.

twenty-two

Mae is a study in patience; she must have been at the wretched yellow house for hours. The arrogance of him to include a return address, confident that it would never be traced in this way. She watches the sun sink behind the hills and listens to the birds preparing to roost for the night. This is madness. What is she going to do to this man? Threaten to do him in with her feeble old fists? What business is it of hers anyway? It is not like January is a silly teenager. She is a grown woman; she can see anyone she wants to. But this man is completely wrong for her, she just can't see it. Mae has to protect January from herself.

A lithe young woman strides up the path with such confidence that she has to live here. More than that, she gives off an air of ownership: it is her home. Although the lights are controlled by sensors, it seems as though her beauty radiates light as they turn on one by one, illuminating each step. The effect is magical, as if all of nature bends to her will. He is married and she must be his wife, but why would he risk losing her for January? Perhaps he knows that he cannot own a woman such as this: January fulfils his need for possession.

'Can I help you?'

'Do you have my tea, dear?'

'Tea?'

'Oh yes, I've been waiting since that girl took my order. Would you bring me a sandwich as well? I'm very hungry now.'

'I don't know what you mean …'

'You should change the light bulbs in here dear. It's awfully dark.'

Another outstanding performance by Mae Raine, who yet again takes a stock character and makes it her very own. Never before has an audience seen a batty old woman played with such intelligence and charisma: Raine brings a humanity to the part that is seldom seen in the work of lesser players.

'How long have you been waiting?'

The young woman uses the clear, distinct voice reserved for foreigners or the deaf. She has impossibly compassionate eyes, and for a moment Mae feels guilty about tricking her, but it must be done to protect January, and perhaps even this girl.

'Since he dropped me off this morning.'

'Who?'

'My nephew, dear. He dropped me off at the tearoom and will pick me up later.'

'From the tearoom?'

'Of course! Otherwise I might get lost; I don't know my way around the city.'

'And you're at the tearoom now?'

'Well, you work here, not me, dear. Could you check on that tea for me?'

'You'd better come inside where it's warm. I'm not sure what to do.'

'It's a good thing you're so pretty if you don't even know how to make a cup of tea.'

The kitchen is one of those modern monstrosities, all chrome and white and impossibly bright. It looks as though it has been tacked on to the rest of the house, an after-thought. When this house was built they wouldn't have dreamed of letting people see the kitchen, the domain of the domestic: particularly in a house of this grandeur. Nowadays kitchens are a display of grotesque wealth, and each guest is ushered in to ooh and ah at the latest appliances and shiny surfaces. This kind of kitchen is not meant to nourish the house; its monochromatic scheme is far too clinical for that.

Indeed the only concession to nature here is a large vase of overblown roses: red of course.

'They're beautiful, aren't they? It was our anniversary yesterday.'

'Anniversary, dear?'

Mae should be listening to what this girl is actually saying. Instead she wonders if her writing stretches out across the page as languidly as each of her syllables. Mae follows, clutching her warm mug of tea, as if the girl is leaving a trail of letters behind her. She shows Mae a photograph of their wedding day, this girl in traditional white, her hair pooling like ink at her shoulders. He is wearing a suit without the awkward self-consciousness Mae sees in most young men today: here is a man confident of his place in the world; a man confident enough to marry and keep a woman as beautiful as this one. For the life of her, Mae can't reconcile this man with the writing in the letters. She knows you can't judge a book ... but something doesn't add up.

'Are you all right?'

'I just feel a little woozy, dear. May I have a glass of water?'

'Just sit there and I'll bring it to you ...'

Mae sits on their substantial couch, her mind tracing and retracing the writing. On the mantle is another vase of roses, red again, and next to them a card. Mae gets that little jump in her stomach, the kind she always gets when a card arrives in the mail. She was hoping to find one today, and – just her luck – she has. The card is a standard anniversary card, probably with a saccharine verse inside filled with cliché, so all he has to do is sign his name to it.

To my Olivia ...

It is clear at a glance that this is not the same author of January's letter. The letters have an even slope, and they do not shy away from the reader like a threatened animal. His forms are rounded and his vowels are open, rather than sneaking and closed off as they are in the letter. This man has nothing to hide: his handwriting is messy but legible; the words are not at odds with his sentiment. There is real emotion here; there is real love.

'He has terrible writing; I'm surprised you can read it.'

Mae folds the card up. She gulps the water Olivia offers her.

'Terrible it may be, Olivia, but not terrible enough.'

Olivia laughs. It is full-bodied: not that irritating stifled giggle that has infected most young women. She begins another anecdote, harmless and amusing, her voice wrapping up Mae's senses like the heady scent from the roses. Surprising, since most roses today are grown to look beautiful but smell of nothing: perfection on the outside but without substance, a facade that masks their real nature. It is the roses that finally confirm Mae's suspicion; red staining white, the sweet smell with an under-note of decay, the erratic writing that seems too much to occur naturally. That writing had been hot-housed, forced into bloom by an impatient hand. The answer is not here: the answer is back at the cottage.

'Thank you for the tea.'

Mae rushes out, ignoring Olivia's plea for patience. She has wasted too much time here. How could she be so blind? His writing was too bad to be true: every deviant trait was present. She should have known; she should have seen. Perhaps January knew that Mae wouldn't be able to resist it; a near-perfect sample demonstrating every evil in humanity. Mae had been blinded by pure worry for the girl: she wanted to protect someone she cared for. If she had paused to think, if she had not taken it at face value, if she had not been so trusting, Mae would have seen the contrivance. Mae feels betrayed: by January and, more troublingly, by her instincts.

The cottage is dark when she arrives home. Cat greets her: weaving in and out of her legs as she walks into the cottage. The sitting room is dully lit by the dying embers in the fireplace, and Mae can see January curled up in a quilt. She touches her head: the hair is damp. January tries to swat away Mae's hand with her own, and Mae catches it. Although January's hand confirms Mae's theory, she is still shocked to see it.

January's hands are perfect: the dryness and cracks that had recently marred the skin have gone. Instead it is as soft and smooth as the cream that feeds it. Absolutely flawless, except for the red ink that stains her fingers and has seeped under her nails.

Disappointment overwhelms Mae. Part of her had still been in denial, didn't want to admit what was patently true. But she can't deny this evidence. She's caught her.

Red-handed.

twenty-three

The fire has been built up when January opens her eyes. It is dark, and her mouth is dry. For a moment she doesn't discern the difference in smell, the slightly acid tang of paper burning instead of the nuttiness of wood. In the blur of residual sleepiness she can see Mae sitting by the fire, calmly feeding the flames. Cat, the little pagan, skips in front of it, occasionally hopping to get the attention of her mistress. But January recognises this posture in Mae. It is as if she has a new sample to examine; nothing will distract her precise movements. January's senses sharpen, and she can make out a tin, her tin, beside Mae. January wants to save the few letters that are left, but a simple flick of Mae's wrist would immolate them all.

'I'm not sure if it was a game for you or not, these letters. Either way, it shows me that you are a little unstable, perhaps not suited for this at all.'

'What do you mean, Mae?'

'I don't think I can teach you any more. I didn't realise how it would affect you.'

'As usual, you're talking in riddles.'

'You do realise that none of it was real, don't you January?'

'Of course it is real. You have the evidence in your hand …'

In a moment of uncharacteristic grace, January snatches a letter from Mae's hand. The paper, the writing: all solid; it is real. It is all here: the proof of her relationship is these letters. The stains on her fingers confuse January, and as she looks at them the letter falls from her hands, like the veil from her eyes.

'You never signed his name.'

January flexes her fingers as if to make sure that she is in control of them. Is this how the freshly exorcised feel? Examining their body for bruises and cuts that they are not responsible for?

'Did you even know his name, January?'

Was the whole thing a fantasy? No, she is not that kind of crazy. It is like a strange plot from a romance novel: this is a test of the heroine's love. She won't deny him. She must remain steadfast in her emotions in order to win him.

'I can't believe this.'

'Some people are more sensitive than others. In some it is a blessing; but many more cannot cope. I should have seen it in you.'

Mae narrows her eyes at January, regarding her carefully, as one would a dangerous animal. She stoops down, not breaking eye contact as she picks up the letter from the ground.

'You can't believe that I'm capable of making something like this up. Do you, Mae?'

'I think you underestimate yourself, January.'

It can't be true. Mae must have gotten it wrong, that's the only logical explanation; although January cannot explain away the red stains on her fingers. She cannot accept that Mae is right; that she has been fooling herself for so long; that what she feels for him is some sort of deceit. January can't stand the way Mae is looking at her: a mixture of disappointment and pity. Why should she care what Mae thinks of her? But she can't even look Mae in the eye. Mae's opinion of her matters because Mae matters. All these years creating an island for herself, and this is what happens. Mae goes and builds a bridge, without resource consent. January's embarrassment colours her cheeks. She balls her hands up into fists, not wanting to see her stained fingers any longer. She wants to hurt Mae. But not physically: she is still in control of her fists. She's not sure why she feels so angry. She isn't even sure if she is mad at Mae or herself.

She'll burn it all. To start with she'll pull down the framed autographs and smash their glass. She wants to yell and scream at Mae, but rage has stolen her voice. She wants to destroy Mae's world as methodically as Mae has done hers. She does the only thing she can think of to bring her life into balance again: she pulls Mae's journal down from the shelf. She wants to rip the pages out one by one, but she feels slightly sick at the thought of it, and her fingers tingle as though the pages are electrified. The ink stains on her hands remind her now of blood. She is Lady Macbeth forced into murder; the insane act will beget her lunacy. It is Old Testament justice: an eye for an eye, a page for a page. If Mae thinks she's mad she may as well live up to her reputation.

'January, stop.'

If she was really mad, the look on Mae's face would please her: her wide eyes and mouth slightly open in astonishment. Mae slowly rises and holds her arms out to January as if she will embrace her.

'Give it back to me, January.'

January presses the journal close to her chest. She can feel her heart beating through the pages, and for a second she believes that it is a living being. She snatches it away from her body, holding it at arm's length. It is close enough to Mae now, and she lunges at it. January, desperate to keep her advantage, pulls it back. She steps closer to the fire, ready to drop the journal in. Mae pleads like a mother for her child: 'Please.'

It only takes a second between her decision to let go and the destruction of Mae's life. If she was really mad, the flames licking the pages would fill her with excitement.

If she was really mad, she would feel nothing as Mae sinks to the ground, the bright flames reflecting over and over in her tear-filled eyes.

'Get out.'

January runs. She runs until her puffs overwhelm her whooping sobs. She runs until her limbs burn with a fire stronger than the one she had sacrificed upon. She runs until she cannot remember the look on Mae's face. But she can't run forever, and as she is bent double trying to catch her breath, the memories catch up with her, push her down and beat her with a vigour she can't defend against.

The motel might have been glamorous once, maybe thirty years ago, but now it is dingy and faded, like it has lost hope. January digs around her bag, looking for her credit card to check in with. She reaches down to the bottom of the bag, where the receipts and the sweet wrappers reign. Her hand emerges again, fingernails dirty with the dust and hair that lurks at the bottom, victoriously clutching her driver's licence.

The clerk is unimpressed with her find, and taps the credit card sign again. January digs in her bag once more.

She places the keys on the bedside cabinet and lies down on the bed. The mattress seems to sink under the weight of her and her feet mess up the perfectly arranged towels. Does she have the patience to wait the few days the situation demands; the few days Mae needs to calm down and see things rationally again? Exhaustion takes a day from her wait, and she wakes in a dark, unfamiliar room. She fills a few more hours with junk food and infomercials, before sleeping once more. It is surprising how tiring sadness can be. She checks her phone: there is one message.

'January? This is Alice. Just wondering if you were coming into work today: you haven't called ... Please call me, OK?'

She wonders why Alice is so apologetic; perhaps she knows what a sorry case January is. Not a word from Mae, nothing.

The next morning she wakes early: she would normally be putting the kettle on for Mae now. She needs supplies to tide her over: at least a toothbrush and a change of underwear. It occurs to her as she brushes her teeth ineffectively with her finger and water that another letter is due today. Another letter that will remind Mae of that awful night; another letter that if Mae finds it first will threaten her plan of reconciliation.

She heads for the post office. Just as she steps inside, her phone rings. She dumps everything out of her bag to find it before she misses the call.

'Mae?'

'Is that you, January? It's Alice.'

So stupid: she should have checked the caller ID.

'Are you coming into work today?'

'I've had another migraine ...'

'Well, you'd better have a doctor's certificate this time.'

'Listen, Alice ... I have to ...'

She makes dry-retching noises before she hangs up, and the only other customer in the post office legs it before she blows. The coast clear, she opens the door to the box.

Her name is not written in Mae's hand, but on a printed label on an envelope. January opens it, and finds a key. She checks the return address, calls the phone number she finds there, and she knows that Mae has not forgiven her, and will probably never forgive her.

The lock-up is not far from the cottage, just a short bus ride through town. It is paid in full to the end of the month. This is what her life amounts to: a three-square-metre cupboard. Alone in the storage locker, her dreams piled haphazardly around her, January cries at her own stupidity. She finally knows that she is homeless and friendless, and it is all her own doing.

twenty-four

There is nothing left of Mae's at the cottage. The things she owns are packed into trunks and are being chauffeured ahead of her. Even Cat has her own private car, where she sleeps dozily, Mae having forced tranquilisers down her throat this morning. She had hidden under the sheets of the ghosted furniture, and Mae had to bribe her out with the promise of mince. The little general begged her to stand her ground, but this is a tactical retreat. There is nothing cowardly about leaving when it is only you against the world.

This is what happens when you leave yourself vulnerable. Mae had always thought that there was something romantic about the manuscript being defenceless. But she thought it would be a force of nature that destroyed it; something elemental. Not a mere girl, drunk on confusion.

A thought that has been nibbling at Mae's ear strikes again, and she catches it between her two fingers and crushes it like a sand-fly. But like a sand-fly it has many sisters just waiting for their turn to sup on Mae, and as she smears one sibling's blood on her palm another is at Mae's ear buzzing again.

The moment the pages of her journal had given themselves up to the fire – curled and drifted up the chimney to see the world for the first time – Mae knew she had lost everything. Her work, her life.

And something else …

Quiet, sand-fly, unless you want to meet the same fate as your sister …

Someone else …

Once again Mae plucks it from her mind and crushes it. She is still too angry to grieve for her now.

Perhaps Mae is already an anachronism. In the future would there be anything more to study? Will there be any fresh samples to harvest? For once she is glad of her mortality; the future is a terrible thing when you know you'll have no place in it.

The train ride lulls Mae into a false sense of comfort. She can fool herself into thinking that she is only visiting; that one day she will leave. But this is the last journey for her. She returns defeated, the last thread of her life fraying.

'Thanks Lady!'

They all chorus, the last syllable stretched and pitchy in that strange sing-song that they seem to teach them at school.

Mae expects that they will all gorge themselves on sugar; the five dollars she has given them will be a distant memory by tomorrow. She could explain that this is her last hurrah; that they should save some of it for a rainy day, or at the very least pace themselves a little. But where's the fun in that? Kids will be kids, and the whole lot will be spent in a few minutes as they load themselves up with armfuls of sweets and biscuits. She feels a little guilty at ruining their dinner and their mothers' evening. There will be sugar highs and lows to deal with, and from the look of it a fair few sore tummies as well.

The house is already open and the kettle is on by the time Mae arrives. As always, it is spotless, with that familiar scent of wax and lavender that makes her feel immediately at home.

Jasmine circles around Mae and pulls her by the hand. 'Mae, Mae! Look at what I drew!'

'Jasmine, at least let her inside. Sorry Mae, she's been jumping around since she heard you were coming.'

'She's fine.'

Cheryl presses her cheek against Mae's and then takes her arm to help her up the step.

'Let me take that bag. I could have picked you up at the station, you know.'

Jasmine is already down the hallway. She turns and puts her hands on her hips.

'Hurry up you two!' She disappears into the kitchen.

Cheryl can't help herself. Her mothering now extends to Mae, who is glad for the tea that is placed near her elbow.

'Here, drink this. You look a little pale.'

'Mae! Mae! Look Mae, I made it for you ...' Jasmine waves a rolled-up piece of paper at Mae. 'You have to open it now!'

'Jasmine, let Mae drink her tea.'

'But it's *important*. I have a secret to tell her.'

Cheryl shrugs at Mae, who waves off her concern.

'What's the secret dear?'

Jasmine leans into Mae and whispers in her ear, 'You were wrong about the letters, Mae ...'

Mae snaps back, spilling her tea on the floor.

Cheryl rushes to Mae's side. 'Mae; are you all right?'

'I was just startled ...'

'What did you say, Jasmine?'

'I just wanted to tell her about the letters, Mummy.'

'Get the cloth for me.' Jasmine knows by her mother's tone not to disobey. 'I'm sorry Mae. I don't know what's gotten into her.'

'It's fine. No harm done.'

Mae sips her tea, and Jasmine arrives back with a dish cloth and a mood just as wet. Mae rummages around her bag dramatically, building anticipation. Finally she unearths it: the tin of sweets they have all expected, the conceit of finding it part of the fun.

'What do you say, Jasmine?'

Jasmine clutches the tin to her chest; she is the youngest, and used to protecting her possessions from the rest of the rabble.

'Thank you.' The voice is treacly and sticky: she has already shoved a small handful in her mouth.

'Don't eat all of them! Take them home and share them with your brothers and sisters. You'd better not ruin your dinner.'

Jasmine runs off. Mae expects she'll eat a few more handfuls before she gets home, to get her fair share. The youngest and the smallest always gets the scraps and leftovers; today she'll get the lion's share.

'You'll spoil them, Mae.'

Mae's chuckle turns into a cough, a loud hacking that she can't disguise as choking. A fresh cup of tea appears, and Mae blinks through teary eyes.

'You're really not well. I should get a doctor.'

'I'm fine. Just tired from the train, I expect. Please don't fuss. I just want to stay at home with my things.'

Cheryl understands this. People around here don't put much stock in hospitals. Better to die at home with your own people than to eke out a few more hours in a sterile ward.

'At least let me help you to bed.'

Mae considers resisting, but she is much too tired for it. A few months ago she would have fought her, fought like she did with January ... but this girl has the strong grip of a mother used to fussy children, and Mae relaxes in her arms.

They slide into the bedroom through a small gap in the door, mindful that Cat may escape, but she is still drowsy from the tranquilisers and confused, and stays under the bed.

'I locked her in here mainly to keep her away from Jasmine. She was dragging the cat around like she was a rag doll.'

In a few hours there is no way Cat will let herself be dragged around. Just give her a little time to regain her senses and her spirit. Mae hopes the same is true for her, but for now she lets Cheryl undress her and help her to bed. Cheryl drags Cat from her hiding place and puts her on the end of the bed. Cat, too dazed by the day, sits where she is told and hesitantly licks her tail.

'Get a bit of rest. I'll wake you for dinner.'

'Thank you.'

As she dozes off, one thought frightens Mae awake. Perhaps this will be the last time: perhaps if she closes her eyes now they'll never open again. But exhaustion wins out as she fights a losing battle with her eyelids. Just a little sleep and she'll be fine.

She wakes with the same confused feeling of disorientation of having slept in a new place. She doesn't know how long she has slept. A few hours at least; the sun has already set. She is aware of two things in this half-sleep state: the weight of the blankets and the sound of Cat mewling at the door, her exhaustion finally worn off. Mae attempts to rise to open the door for her, but finds her own exhaustion is just beginning to settle in.

Cheryl has an uncanny sixth sense; Mae can hear her at the door. She opens it a crack, shooing Cat away.

'I'm going to turn on the light.'

The light makes Mae squint. She is blinded but her other senses work fine; she can smell tea and food as Cheryl brings them to her.

Cheryl fusses with the pillows and the tray before she sweeps Cat up into her arms.

'I expect you need to go to the toilet Cat. I'll lock her in the bathroom while you eat. Be quiet, Cat.'

'Thank you.'

'Not at all. I feel like I'm finally earning what you pay me. I've always felt a little guilty at the amount you pay for a little dusting.'

'Some people wouldn't.'

'It's a good thing that you picked the right person then.'

Mae looks at her soup, thoughts of January suddenly dampening her appetite. How could she have been so wrong?

'Eat up before it gets cold. I'll get rid of Cat and come and keep you company.'

'I can feed myself, thank you.'

'Oh, I know that. I just don't want you to start talking to yourself, eh?'

Cheryl comes back with her own mug of tea. She tells Mae about the news of the town: the same stories but with different players – who has been born, who has left and who has died. Mae lets the words seep into her like ink in paper. The thought of ink makes her gasp a little, the pain of loss still too new. It is as if January murdered her that day. Mae the graphologist has gone, and this is all that is left. Nothing left to do but prepare for death.

'Too hot?'

'What dear?'

'The soup. Too hot?'

'No, it's fine. You don't have to sit with me; I guess you have things to do at home.'

'They can take care of themselves; the eldest would have put dinner on by now. Actually it's quite nice to have a sit-down and a cuppa. I can visit a couple of times a day, morning and night. Lunch, we'll have to sort something out. Maybe I'll send Jasmine over with a cut lunch and thermos.'

'You really needn't go to all this trouble; I'll be fine in the morning.'

'Mae, there are only two reasons people come to this town. They are born here, or they come back to die. I'm guessing you didn't bring that demon of a cat for a holiday.'

Mae notices the fresh red scratches on Cheryl's arms. Cat can be strong when she wants to be. Mae thanks her stars that she had been tranquilised before Mae attempted to put her in her cage.

'I'll pay you extra, of course.'

'Mae, I've known you since you used to give me lolly money, and you gave me this job, which is clearly unnecessary. I clean after you a couple of times a year and yet there's a cheque every week. But it's not the money. You're pretty much family, as far as I can see.'

Mae didn't expect this: Cheryl's speech or the strange stir of her own emotions. She would like to put it down to the stress of the past few days, but it is something deeper. She is scared; scared that she hasn't anything to tie her to this world when she has gone. She knows how tenuous a ghost's grasp is on this world: only the living can keep them here; once their attention is gone so is the ghost. The manuscript was her only stab at immortality, having never passed her genes on to another. Mae wonders what it is like for this girl, knowing that her memory will live on in so many. Would it give you a better grip on the world; make more of a mark than the faint drips of ink of Mae's ghosts? She doesn't notice the tears on her cheeks until Cheryl gently wipes them away.

'There is no shame in asking for help, Mae.'

twenty-five

January's heart beats too hard for sleep tonight. If she closes her eyes she will see her monstrous act played over and over, the memory sharpened over the intervening days and perpetually caught in a loop. She knows there will be no sleep for her in the little night that is left. Her room is too small, so she leaves and walks around the city. She wears his coat with the collar pulled up as protection against the stubborn cold, which lingers despite the change in season. The brush of the collar irritates her skin, but the lust she once felt at its touch has been replaced by shame.

It is to make amends that she sits in her tree, picking the new green growth and waiting for the world to wake up. She counts the steps up to the yellow house like they are beads on a rosary, over and over again. Finally the birds begin to chatter and the street is lit by both the street lamps and the sun.

She is at the bottom of the steps when she hears the slam of a door.

'Where are you going?' Olivia's voice is shaky.

His words are tight. 'To work.'

'You always …' Their argument has raised the pitch of Olivia's voice to whining.

'What? What do I always do, Olivia?'

They are on the steps now. Olivia is wrapped in an old dressing gown; her perfect skin is blotched red with unhappiness. He has his back to January as he argues with Olivia. At first January doesn't recognise him; he looks smaller, his hair thinning slightly at the crown. He holds his keys tightly in his fist.

It is a mundane thing: an argument that will be forgotten by that evening. Once their fighting would have thrilled January; she would have seen it as a crack that she could slowly seep into and use to eventually force them apart. But today she realises that she feels pity for them, and their small, imperfect human lives, and is shocked that it knots her stomach so.

Her argument with Mae must have been like this: tears and choked words. If people could see themselves arguing, it would be impossible for them to keep a straight face: anger would melt into laughter. All would be forgiven.

He looks down at her, and for what she realises is the first time January looks into his eyes. Surprise has coloured them differently. Then it gives way to something else, something that makes January break her gaze. He is regarding her with the contempt he would regard something he has stepped in. He instinctively backs up slowly towards Olivia, and their argument is forgotten in the face of a common enemy.

'Who are you? What are you doing here?'

'She's wearing your coat.' Olivia's voice is strangled by fear.

January pulls the coat's collar up and the sleeves down, trying to disappear like a turtle in its shell.

His words are slow and deliberate; January can almost see them in the chill of the morning air.

'Where did you get that?'

'It's your coat! Look at it.'

'Olivia! Just keep calm …'

'Calm? Who is she?'

Olivia hits his arm. It is an accusation.

'I don't know.'

'Who are you? Who Are You!'

He points at January. 'You. Stay where you are.'

January wonders what he would do if she took a step towards them …

'I'm warning you; don't move.'

January climbs the steps slowly, until there are only a few left between them.

'Olivia, get inside.'

His tone is harsh. Olivia nods and backs into the doorway. It is not until the door clicks shut that he speaks again.

'What do you want?'

He looks shorter, and January doubts whether his arms could span her waist, let alone swing her into a tree. She is disappointed at how quickly he has diminished.

Let me see as I used to …

Her eyes have been shut. She slowly opens them to see him as he is: not the man of her dreams but a poor facsimile, a photocopy copied again and again until the toner has smudged out all recognisable features.

'You're just …' She reaches out to touch his cheek and he pulls away; her fingers land on his arm – solid and real.

'You're just … you.' January pulls her arm away, suddenly aware of the trespass.

His voice softens as if he is placating an angry child. 'Are you in trouble? Is there someone we should call? Will they be missing you?' His smile is indulgent, but his eyes are hard with caution.

'I'm not … I'm not mad. I wouldn't do anything to hurt you.' Wouldn't she? 'I just …'

She feels foolish in his coat. She looks at the sleeves fraying at the hemline, the body which has lost all shape. She can feel the greasy collar rubbing at her neck, and she is repulsed by it all: the unwashed musty smell of it, her sweat and his mingling in its fibres. The suggestion of adultery is dishonest. She strips it off, happy for the cold that snaps at her skin, and leaves it discarded like road-kill on the steps.

He moves the coat back towards her with his foot. 'You can keep it. I think you need it more than I do.'

The door opens, surprising them both. Olivia shakes the phone at January like a tamer trying to subdue a tiger.

'I've called the police.'

January turns and runs.

The wind picks up as she runs downhill to the city; the buildings create a wind tunnel. She pushes forward, half hoping that the sound of sirens will drown out her ragged breath, and their words play over and over in her head.

Who are you?

She slows down; there are no sirens pursuing her. Perhaps she imagined …

No. The fear on Olivia's face was real. The look of pity in his eyes was real.

The morning sun, blocked out by the high-rises, does little to ward off the chill that goose-pimples January's skin. Perhaps she was too hasty in throwing away the coat. It would, after all, fit in perfectly with her new lifestyle as a homeless person. Will she become someone to be avoided; side-stepped in the street, raving at whoever is unlucky enough to be in her vicinity? People are already looking at her out of the corner of their eyes, assessing the threat of her. She folds her arms tighter around her body and quickens her pace. It is too crowded here for her thoughts, too claustrophobic.

She is running again. If it were not for the way she is dressed, she might be mistaken for one of the joggers she overtakes. She runs until the buildings run short, and so does her breath. She stands in the lee of the band rotunda looking at the harbour: a view that the houses above paid millions for.

She is back where she started – alone on this deserted beach. If only she could wipe the slate clean again; erase all her mistakes.

Tabula rasa.

She takes off her shoes and hides them under her bag. The first bite of cold water wraps her skirt around her legs, hobbling her. She flops into the water. Her eyes, open, sting with salt. Her mouth, open from the shock of the cold, is filled with sea water, and the impact forces her to swallow. Her body protests, and her stomach seizes. She drags herself back onto the sand and vomits.

She collapses on the hard sand and lies on her back with her eyes closed, to block out the sun that has risen and to stop her head from spinning. Her mouth is dry and her throat burns with salt and stomach acid. The cramps in her stomach subside, and she considers another mouthful just to feel something real again.

Is the cold that pricks her skin not real? January shivers. Spring mornings are brisk and windy; bad enough when you have a coat to protect against gusts – a coat! She scrunches her eyes, trying to forget the scene, but she can remember every word. Blessed be the mad, for they do not remember – or, more likely, do not care.

The cottage is not far from here; she could show Mae how devastated she is. What could be more pathetic than January soaked to the skin on your doorstep? Mae wouldn't let her die of exposure; she would let January in, and then she would explain and everything would be fine again. Mae will forgive her, she's sure. Even though she had destroyed her life's work.

In her eyes the cottage has diminished; it shies away from the buildings that surround it like a wounded animal hunched low to the ground.

She turns the key in the lock and berates herself for not having practised what she is going to say.

The cottage has a different feel about it, which she cannot place until she realises that Cat hasn't attacked her legs with affection. She finally notices the sheets on the furniture. She refuses to accept the obvious, checking each room. But Mae has gone.

At first, January thinks she must be in shock; her whole body seems to be shaking. She looks at her hands: they are pale and her fingernails are a little blue. She walks to the bathroom and looks in the mirror. Her lips are tinged blue with cold. She turns on the shower and steps under the hot water fully clothed, stripping off as the numbness in her limbs retreats. The fresh water dissolves the salt that has dried on her face, and it drips down her cheeks and nose like …

Her crocodile tears are replaced with real ones. She is alone. When Mae told her to leave, she had him. When he wasn't real, she thought she'd have Mae. Now the worst thing is her realisation is that she has done it all to herself. She invented the affair with him and she destroyed her relationship with Mae because of it; because she refused to accept … what? She can't get her head around it, let alone accept it. But she can't deny it any more either; the truth. She is still shaking, even though she is warmed through. She is still shaking as she climbs out of the shower; as she dries and wraps herself in a towel.

She lands in a heap on Mae's chair, unable to control the sobs that shake her. Funny: she hasn't cried as much in her entire life as she has in the past week. It is here that the horrific thought hits her. What if she had imagined Mae, just as she had done with him? She scrambles in her bag and pulls out the manuscript, hoping to be comforted by its presence, but feels more confused. Perhaps this isn't real either. January remembers the letters and the red ink twisting around her fingers. No, not again. Mae's life had been too rich, too foreign to be the stuff of imagination; Mae must be real because constructing her would be far too much work for a slacker like January.

Satisfied that Mae is real, January wonders where she could be. Then an equally frightening thought grips her. Perhaps this time Mae really has …

Euphemisms escape her. If you don't actually say the word then it can't be true. It can't be true. Someone would have called her, told her. But why would they? She was an assistant; it is not as if she was *family*.

She wills herself to think: who would know for sure the fate of Mae? Who could she call? No one in the city. No, not the city … and then she realises where Mae would go. Mae would go home; back to the place she left so readily all those years ago.

January runs down the stairs and grabs her bag, digging for the small card Mae had written the address on. She tips the bag on the floor, searching through every receipt and wrapper that has been composting slowly at the bottom of it. It is not there, even when she checks the scraps of paper one by one before dropping them into the fireplace.

It looks so harmless now: an empty black hole. Mae must have cleared the ashes January wonders if she gave them a burial or scattered them to the wind. It had been more than a journal to Mae:

it was her life. January looks at her replica journal on the floor, the leather cover already wrinkled at the spine. It seems wrong to call it hers: none of the thoughts within belong to January. She opens it and sees again the familiar hand of Mae – albeit a little less sure and a little more shaky. The stupidity of her destruction is matched only by the stupidity of her salvation. So many days wasted. Is this how Dorothy felt when she found out that she could have gone home; that she had the answer all along?

To rub salt in, the card she has been looking for falls out of the pages.

There's no place like ...

January feels giddy with hope as she rings the car rental place: that she will find Mae; and that perhaps Mae will even forgive her, if she is not too late.

It is late afternoon by the time she has organised her journey. She had to wait at the cottage for her clothes to dry before she could pack up her things at the motel, and then, annoyingly, her body demanded food; as if she hadn't eaten in the past twelve hours. Each bite wasted precious time.

Her phone rings a few times, but she doesn't answer when she sees that it is Alice. There's nothing she could say to Alice now anyway. She turns her phone off.

Driving out of the city, she makes one last stop. The earth under the tree is soft and easy to dig, as if it is ready to give up her secret. It must be a strange scene for those passing by: January on her knees digging like an animal.

She smiles, imagining herself as the star of an amusing anecdote.

You won't believe what I saw on the way home, dear! Just under the tree, scratching out the dirt ... An office worker gone feral.

The scarf has long since gone and the lid is rusty, but the jar is intact. It sits next to January on her journey, and feels as if it is a real passenger, its presence is so great.

January reaches over and pats it, reassuring it that she remembers how to drive; that they will get there safely.

It will be a long drive, with just you and me.

She switches on the stereo and turns it up to drown out the thump of her heart, the nag of her brain. She needs to concentrate on just getting there, and not what will happen once she is. For once January can see the virtue of living in the now, and drives with just the thought of the asphalt a few metres ahead of her.

twenty-six

Mae awakes to find the corner of the bedspread thrown over the top of the bed. If she moves slightly over she can see two small legs, clothed in denim that has seen better days, kicking like Jasmine is trying to swim across the floor. She succeeds and disappears another inch under the bed. Mae rolls back and tries to decipher whether this is a dream. That is when she sees a sandwich on a plate, cling-film around the whole package, and a thermos on the bedside table. She moves again, this time making sure the child underneath will feel the movement. The legs stop kicking, and she can imagine Jasmine's head tilted, waiting for confirmation that she's awake. Mae coughs a little, and Jasmine's legs scramble backwards. Mae rolls back and pretends that she's just been roused. Jasmine, for her part, pretends that she has been standing at the end of the bed; the cover has once again been straightened.

'Mum said not to wake you.'

'You didn't wake me.'

Jasmine is relieved.

'She said that I should leave your lunch and then come home.'

She makes no move to leave.

'You can stay here with me and help me with my lunch. We could have a picnic.'

Jasmine nods, and Mae unwraps the sandwich. From the front

pocket of her bibbed trousers she pulls out the tin of sweets Mae gave her, and places it carefully on the bed. Mae hands Jasmine a sandwich half, and she takes a huge bite from the middle, spreading its contents across her cheeks. She swings her legs off the side of the bed; her legs make small judders on the frame as they hit.

'Jasmine, why are you here?'

'I want to pat her.'

'Who? Cat?'

She nods, and Mae understands what she had been doing. Cat probably has backed herself into the corner away from little hands. Mae expects if she let Jasmine get any closer she would see scratches on her hands to match her mother's.

'Cat is not very friendly at the moment. I think you should leave her alone until she gets to know you.'

'That's what Mum said.'

Mae nibbles at the corner of her sandwich. Jasmine chomps through hers as if she is trying to eat as quickly as she can, to get to the sweets.

'I thought those sweets would be gone by now.'

Jasmine grins and shakes her head. She opens her mouth to speak, before Mae censures her.

'Don't speak with your mouth full.'

The child makes a big show of chewing, and swallows with a big gulp. She is almost breathless with the effort.

'I hid them from the others.'

'Where?'

Jasmine grins and shakes her head, before taking a huge mouthful of sandwich. Mae can tell what she is thinking from that cheeky look on her face.

I can't talk with my mouth full, that's what you said ...

Butter wouldn't melt as they say.

'Jasmine, what were you trying to tell me yesterday?'

Jasmine shakes her head. 'You'll get upset.'

'No I won't.'

'Mummy says it's rude to tell someone they're wrong, but she tells me when I'm wrong all the time.'

'She's trying to teach you right from wrong.'

'But that's all I wanted to do, 'cos you got it wrong.'

'What did I get wrong?'

Jasmine runs off to the kitchen and brings back the rolled-up piece of paper she had tried to give Mae the day before.

'This.'

Mae pushes herself up in the bed. Jasmine has copied the alphabet as Mae had written it, but each letter is in a different shade. The colour is more striking than the uncontrolled size and curves of the letters that give away Jasmine's age.

'You were wrong about the letters Mae, see?' Jasmine points to each letter. 'None of them is black.'

Mae gives Jasmine a squeeze. 'Has anyone ever told you that you are fascinating, Miss?'

Mae traces the letters, so familiar yet new again.

'Do you know what colour your name is, Jasmine?'

Jasmine shakes her head.

'Do you want to find out?'

'I don't know how to draw my name.'

'I can teach you that, but I need you to get me a few things. You'll need to be very brave. Are you a brave girl?'

Jasmine nods her head slowly.

'No. I think maybe you're too little …'

'No! I'm a big girl!'

'You'll have to do some pretending. Are you good at pretending?'

Jasmine solemnly nods her head, hanging off Mae's every word.

'You see my hat and coat? You need to take those and put them on. Yes? You look very smart, Jasmine. Now you need to pretend that you're me.'

Mae hadn't realised that she moved so slowly or looked as feeble to the rest of the world.

'Did you see me? Did you see me, Mae?'

'Yes, I saw you. But you'll have to pretend for much longer than that. Now you need to go to the end of the hall to the sitting room, do you know where that is? Good. Go to the desk in the sitting room and bring me some paper and a pen.'

'Why do I need to dress up?'

'Because if they think you are me they won't hurt you.'

'Who?'

'The ghosts.'

'There's no such thing as ghosts. Me and Mum go in there all the time.'

'Of course you wouldn't see them with your mother. They wait until little girls are all by themselves and poof! They take you away.'

'Where?'

'Nobody knows, because you never come back.'

'I don't want to go in there …'

'You'll be perfectly safe in the hat and coat. The ghosts don't want an old woman like me.'

The child pulls the hat further down on her head.

'Just go straight to the desk and don't touch anything else. We don't want to upset them.'

Jasmine gives a little nod and creeps out the door.

Mae has finished the thermos of tea when the child comes back.

Cat, comfortable now at the end of the bed, considers legging it, but decides to hold her ground. Mae strokes her as Jasmine approaches.

'Look who is out for a visit.'

The child hands over the paper and pen, and quietly climbs onto the bed. Cat raises herself to a crouch, expecting the rough treatment of yesterday, but Jasmine, subdued by her ordeal, only pats her gently. Cat begins to purr hesitantly, and then abandons all her fears, even rolling on her back for a tummy scratch. That cat is shameless some days.

Mae writes Jasmine's name in big rounded letters. She has to help Jasmine hold the pen and form the shapes for the first couple of tries. After that Jasmine shrugs off Mae's help and practises happily on the floor.

The sweet in Mae's mouth has dissolved to nothing by the time Jasmine shows her the copy she is most proud of.

'I need my pens to do it properly, Mae.'

She holds it out so Mae can see, her little fingers framing the sides. Each of the fingers on her right hand has been blotched with ink, and for the first time this afternoon Mae is reminded of why she came back.

'Have I done it wrong, Mae?'

The little voice is on the point of breaking itself.

'No, it's very good, Jasmine. It looks just like mine.'

'Then why are you crying?'

'It just reminded me of a sad story.'

'Is there a princess in the story?'

'Of sorts. Her name is January.'

'That's a funny name.'

'She was a funny princess. But it wasn't her real name.'

'What was her real name?'

'Nobody knew but her. But over time she had forgotten it too. So she would write and write names trying to find the right one. She wrote so much that her fingers became stained with ink.'

'Like mine?'

'Just like yours. That's why you reminded me.'

'Perhaps January needs someone to remind her too. Then she would know who she is.'

'That is very clever. Have you heard this story before?'

'No. Tell me the story, Mae.'

Jasmine settles in closer to Mae, propped up against the pillow. What harm is there in telling the child? Dressed up as a fairytale, their story will be mixed up with pigs and wolves, skin as fair as snow and hair that tumbles from a tower to the ground. Perhaps there was a kernel of truth in them all, forgotten through time. Perhaps in this small way Mae will live on.

'This is a long story, that can't be told in one day. You'll have to come back to hear the rest, all right?'

'Yes, Mae.'

'Then this story begins in a small cottage …'

'Once upon a time.'

'What?'

'That's how they start. Once upon a time.'

'Once upon a time, in a small cottage much like this one, a girl was born …'

twenty-seven

When January arrives at the Raine house a gaggle of children, costumed in old sheets and hand-me-down ball gowns, passes by with pillow slips filled with sweets. January wonders if she should join them in trick-or-treating; she certainly feels monstrous enough. On this night of the year, at least in the northern hemisphere, the veil between the worlds is thin. January had hoped this would work to her advantage; that she could easily slip back into Mae's world. She has not expected the difficulty of her task. Standing on the threshold is a woman, probably not that much older than her, but older in experience, in real life. Her hands, broadened and toughened with real work – skin-splitting, fingernail-destroying work – rest on her hips, broadened too by work, or perhaps by the little one clinging to her leg and the rest of her brood.

She had opened the door widely and stood square in the frame: so unlike January, used to peeking through cracks that are chained for safety.

'Whadda you want?'

She speaks with the sharpness of consonants rounded off, with as little movement as possible in her mouth; it is as if her words are formed somewhere deeper. Indeed, they seem to resonate despite her mouth only being open a fraction. It is at once intimidating and comforting: January has not been in the city long enough to forget the slight nod of friendship in these parts. The better you know someone the less you say; the mark of true friendship is nothing but the raise of an eyebrow.

'The guy at the pub said this was the Raine house.'

'Did he now.'

She doesn't move. Her child moves a little from behind her, and January can see that, held in her small arm, tucked into her armpit like a rag doll, is the pleading face of Cat. January drops down to child level.

'Hello, Cat.'

The mother instinctively moves in front of her child, who in a moment that seems suspended in time drops Cat from her grasp. Cat drops to the ground, already running.

'Ah! That blimmin' cat. I told you to hold on to it.'

The child immediately begins to bawl, and January stands awkwardly in the doorway, unsure whether to offer help or to look away.

'Go and look for the cat before it heads to the bush.'

January is so relieved to be released that she is a few hundred steps away before she realises that she has taken orders from a complete stranger. Not only that, but the woman probably wasn't even talking to her. She was probably talking to her daughter. No matter: she has to find Cat. She can't be responsible for losing another thing that matters so much to Mae.

The Raine house is further out of town than the rest of the houses. It had seemed to January as she drove through the streets that the other houses had secrets to share with each other, but had turned their back on the Raine house. It was like the outcast in an eighties teen movie: one good makeover and the rest of the houses would welcome it into their town. January wonders which of Mae's great grandfathers had chosen the spot. From here she can see that it looks over the town paternally; it is there to protect the rest of the houses it reigns over.

Raine, reign.

And then it begins to rain.

It is not long before January, voice hoarse from calling, is soaked to the bone. She has checked every cat-sized hole, every bush along this road. Presuming Cat came along the road. She silently curses her fallible human logic. Cat could be anywhere; she could have gone in any direction: most unlikely is the nice road. What did she expect? To find Cat waiting for her at the end of the drive? To come out to meet her in this weather?

Cat had found a nice dry spot in the crawl space. She could hear the child bawling and the mother attempting to calm her. She had heard the clump, clump of January running down the road and her name being called. Cat cleans her tail as she feels the change in air pressure, and is glad she has found a nice place to snooze before the rain sets in.

The front door is locked, and January follows the veranda that wraps around the house to a lean-to kitchen. The door is open, and January can see the woman at the table nursing a cup of tea.

'I didn't find her.' January inches closer to the door, waiting to be invited in.

The child sits at the table as well, her eyes swollen red with crying, her unsteady breath hinting that any small thing will set her off again. She clutches a cup, the tea barely colouring the milk.

'Cat will come back when she's hungry.' As she tells the girl, January hopes that it is true. 'You don't get a tummy like that from missing any meals.'

The child looks to her mother for confirmation, and the woman nods, grateful for the little help January has offered. The child breaks out into a relieved grin and happily slurps her tea.

'Thank you, January.'

'How did you …'

'Mae hasn't stopped talking about you. And who else would come up here looking for her? I haven't lost all my brains to babies you know.'

'I need to talk to Mae.'

'I don't think that would be a good idea, do you?'

She stands and rests her hand on the kitchen door. 'I've arranged a room at the hotel for you. Say that Cheryl sent you and they'll look after you.'

January stands still; unsure what to do. 'I just want to tell her …'

'You'd better go to the hotel and change out of those wet clothes before you catch a cold.' Cheryl pauses before she shuts the door completely. 'You can stop by tomorrow; we'll see if she wants to talk to you then.'

If her motel room in the city had looked like it had lost hope thirty years ago, this room looks like it had given up twenty years before that. January sits under the bedcover, her hair still wrapped in a towel. She had taken a long bath in the shared bathroom down the hall; she was the only guest here tonight, so no one disturbed her. Being the only guest has already made her infamous – everyone in the pub downstairs knew who she was and why she was here when she had said that Cheryl had sent her.

She had felt their eyes on her as she dripped on the carpet that smelt of stale beer and cigarettes of the distant past. She had turned around when she heard 'Raine', but couldn't be sure if they were talking about her or the weather. She decides to stay in her room tonight, despite the hunger gnawing her stomach.

She can't sleep again. Just as she is about to drop off, the thought of what she has done jars her awake. She lies in bed for an hour before she gets up and dresses quietly. She leaves the rental car in the hotel car park; Mae's house is only a short walk from here. January is surprised how much warmer it is here than Wellington: probably only one or two degrees, but the lack of wind chill makes a huge difference. By the time she reaches Mae's house she has unbuttoned her coat completely.

Jasmine runs ahead of her mother. She wants to get to the fence at Mae's house before her mother gets there so she can climb over by herself. But as she approaches the fence, she can see someone at the back door, and she runs back to her mother.

'Mummy! There's someone at Mae's!'

January sits by the kitchen door, her hooded jacket pulled around her. Cheryl nudges her awake and away from the door, and unlocks it. 'You're here early.'

January moves stiffly; it was colder last night than she thought. 'I know the hours Mae keeps.'

Cheryl offers her hand to January to pull her to her feet. January feels ashamed of her smooth pampered hand when she takes Cheryl's: ashamed of all the times she has complained about how hard she has worked sitting at her desk wasting time. Cheryl has no time to waste; every minute must be accounted for. January wonders if it is a relief to have your life mapped out, free of the worry that a decision may be the wrong one. The fact that she has children amazes January: that she seems not to be racked by the torture of sacrificing something of yourself. Presuming that Cheryl had a choice in the matter. For once it occurrs to January that she's privileged, rather than cursed, by choice.

'You may as well come in and help me with the tea while I light the fire then.'

The wood range quickly warms both January and the kettle upon it. Cheryl makes three cups of tea for Jasmine, January and herself in mugs. Mae's teapot is warmed and the tea leaves measured in, and it is filled with water. Cheryl pours the tea into a porcelain cup decorated with forget-me-nots.

'I'll take this to Mae and tell her you're here, January. You finish off our tea: milk and one sugar for me, plenty of milk and a little sugar for Jas.'

The child grins and pokes her small tongue at January. January is sorely tempted to poke her tongue back, but screws up her nose at the child instead. The child whoops in victory over the strange lady. Her mother looks at her and she settles again.

'If you can't be quiet, Jasmine, you can go and have your tea in the sitting room.'

'By myself?'

'If you can't be quiet …'

'But I can't Mummy, there's ghosts …'

'Who told you there were ghosts?'

'Mae did. She said if I go in there and touch anything the ghosts would come out and …'

January smiles as she stirs the tea.

Crafty old Mae.

'Well, you had better behave while I'm gone then, hadn't you?'

Mae is sitting up in her bed when Cheryl enters with tea.

'So she's here.'

'Who?' Cheryl feigns ignorance as she pours Mae's tea.

'You know very well who, Cheryl. I'm not deaf, you know. I heard you two chattering.'

'She says she has something to tell you.'

'Well, I don't care to listen to what she has to say.'

Cheryl comes back to the kitchen and shakes her head. 'What did you do?'

January wants to tell her, but she knows that Cheryl wouldn't let her back in the house if she did.

'Great.' Cheryl puts her hands on her hips. 'Silence from the pair of you. I hope you're as stubborn as Mae is, because she's not budging.'

No matter. January has decided that she can wait for Mae; she only hopes that Mae can wait for her. To pass the time she helps Cheryl with the cleaning, dusting a little here and there until Cheryl the dynamo shoos her off to sit in the kitchen and keep out of the way. It turns out she is more use in the kitchen anyway keeping Jasmine amused.

At first Jasmine seems a little afraid of January. January expects it is because she is so old to someone so small. Until Jasmine pipes up.

'Are you the princess in the story?'

'What story?'

'The one Mae is telling me.'

'Can you tell me the story, Jas?'

The child thinks on this and nods.

'I'm going to help you, January.'

'How are you going to help me, Jasmine?'

'I'll tell you the story tomorrow. I'm going to make you remember.'

That night January heads back to the hotel and checks her phone: one missed call from Alice.

'January, this is Alice. Look, if you're not in tomorrow ... you may as well not come in. Your final written warning is on your desk. Call me back and I'll try and ... I don't know what ... Just call back, OK?'

Looks like January has plenty of time to spare for Mae.

She heads down to the pub and orders a glass of bubbly.

The man at the bar grins at her as he pours. 'Celebration, eh?'

January drains half the glass. 'No, I've just lost my job.'

The man stops smiling. 'Crikey. I thought ... well, most people order this when they're happy.'

'And who's to say I'm not?'

'The way Cheryl tells it ...'

Bloody small towns.

She grabs the bottle of wine. 'I'll take this to my room, if that's OK.'

The next morning Jasmine can't wait to tell January the story. She whines as her mother bustles the other children into clothes for school, cuts lunches and sips her tea.

'C'mon Mummy. We'll be late.'

Jasmine runs ahead of her, impatiently turning back to her mother with her hands on her hips.

'All right, Jas. I'm coming. Taihoa.'

January is waiting at the kitchen door again. She winces as Jasmine shouts her hellos.

'Feeling a bit delicate this morning?' Cheryl helps January to her feet.

'I'm fine.'

'Look, Jimmy told me you lost your job.'

'Who's Jimmy?'

'The barman, my husband ... Jas! Inside voice, please. He also told me you had a few last night.'

'But Mummy! I need to tell January ...'

'Not now, Jas.'

'But MUMMY!'

'Jasmine! Time out in the sitting room. Now.'

Jasmine hangs around by the kitchen door.

'Now, Jasmine.'

Jasmine walks down the hall, dragging her feet and her bottom lip behind her.

'You know Mae has been telling her ghost stories. Maybe she should have her time out in here.'

'She needs to learn ...'

'Make her apologise. Look, I'm saving you loads of money in therapy later on.'

Cheryl walks into the sitting room to find her youngest daughter sitting bolt upright in the middle of the couch with her hands clamped over her eyes.

'What are you doing, love?'

The voice that replies is so tiny that Cheryl has to lean close to her daughter; Jasmine's breath warms her cheek.

'The ghosts can't see me if I can't see them.'

Cheryl bites her lip to stop laughing and stores this moment away for an excruciating twenty-first story.

'C'mon, take my hand. I'll lead you out.'

Jasmine complies, her eyes screwed up.

'Is it safe yet, Mummy?'

'Yes. You can open your eyes now. You can go and sit in the kitchen, but you have to say sorry to January.'

'I just wanted to tell her a story ...'

'January's not feeling well.'

'Like Mae?'

'Not quite. January will be better soon.'

January sips her tea in the kitchen.

'Mummy says you're sick.'

'Just feeling a little sorry for myself.'

'Why?'

January looks to Cheryl, who shrugs. 'Tell you the truth, January, I'd like to know myself.'

'I've done some stupid things and hurt some people.'

'Mummy says that it's more helpful to talk than to hit.'

'That's good advice. But that's not the kind of hurt I meant.'

'I'm sorry, January.'

'I am too, Jas.'

'I'll make up the spare room for you.' Cheryl is already washing their tea cups.

'I'm fine at the hotel.'

'You can't afford the hotel. You've lost your job, remember?'

'I'll just stay there until Mae comes around …'

'We both know that could be a long while. There's plenty of room here. When Mae finds out about the situation, she'll insist on it.'

January raises her eyebrow.

'All right. But I'm sure she will when she comes to her senses.'

'No Cheryl,' Mae folds her arms. 'She absolutely cannot stay here.'

Cheryl hears the crunch of the driveway gravel. January is back from the hotel already.

'She has nowhere else to go.'

'There's the hotel. She could stay with you.'

'Where would she sleep at my house? You have a perfectly good room to spare here. What did she do that was so bad? Was it bad enough to forget about how people are around here, Mae? That we help someone when they're in trouble?'

Mae pouts, and for a second looks like Jasmine when she sulks.

'She's not to come into my room under any circumstance.'

'Understood, Mae. Now, do you need another cuppa?'

That night after Cheryl has left for her own home, January hovers outside Mae's door. She peeks through the gap in the door, left probably so Cat can come in and out.

Bloody Cat. I'd forgotten about you.

Mae seems dwarfed by the bed, hardly large in itself. January wonders if she destroyed more than the manuscript that day. More than a friendship. January wonders if she has destroyed Mae as well.

Every day January looks forward to Jasmine's visits. In a way she can fool herself that she is talking to Mae. Jasmine has become a go-between, a conduit for the women. Mae still stubbornly refuses to talk to January. In the afternoons when Jasmine is in Mae's room, January sits with her back against the door, like she did in the city, listening to their soft voices. When she can no longer stand it she goes out for a walk, looking for Cat, who is surely halfway to Wellington by now, but she still shakes the cat biscuits in any small hole likely to be a hideout.

'Hi January! Are you ready?'

'Morning Jas. Sit up at the table while I say hello to your Mum.'

January pours another two cups of tea. One is in the sturdy mug that follows Cheryl around the house, and the other in delicate china with matching saucer. She hands both to Cheryl.

'You should take it to her yourself.'

'We both know how that would end.'

'January, come on! I can't hold the story in!'

'Are bits falling out your ears, Jas?'

'Don't be silly, January.'

But Jasmine checks the floor, just in case.

Cheryl sighs in relief when the two of them have finally settled down and she can clean in peace. Sometimes when they're engrossed she'll slip back into Mae's room for a chat.

'I don't want to hear it.'

'I'm not here to plead January's case. I'm just here to dust.'

'Good.'

'She just wants to make it up to you, and she came all this way ...'

'And she can go all the way back.'

'C'mon Mae, we both know you're aching to see her. At least to see what she's brought with her.'

'What has she brought?'

'You'll just have to ask her, won't you?'

There is nothing January can give Mae that she can possibly want. The two things she treasured in this world have gone by January's hand: the first deliberately and the second by stupidity. Of course in January's case that could be deliberate as well.

The next day there is no excitement in Jasmine. She mopes into the kitchen and sits heavily at the table. January looks at Cheryl, who just shrugs.

'Are you OK, Jas?'

'No.'

'Why not?'

'Because there's none left. Mae didn't have any story left, and now I don't know what happens in the end.'

'Hmm. Do you know what has happened?'

Jasmine tilts her head in curiosity at January, and shakes her head.

'The story has caught up with us. We're in the middle of the story.'

'It doesn't look like a story, January.'

'That's because you have to look harder.'

Jasmine screws up her eyes and looks around the room.

'It still doesn't look like a story.'

'Wait here.'

January leaves Jasmine, face still tense trying desperately to see the fiction around her.

It seems like forever since January left. Jasmine has tried everything to see the story. She has closed one eye and then the other; she has looked through her lashes, but she still hasn't seen it. Maybe January was wrong. Maybe she's as 'muddle brained' as Mae said, whatever that means. Jasmine isn't sure what Mae means sometimes, and when that happens she asks January what Mae means, but the way January explains it can be even more confusing. Maybe it's because she can't see the story. Maybe the story has been happening all this time and she's missed it. Jasmine hates missing out on anything; her brothers and sisters always leave her out of things because she's 'too little'.

'C'mon, Jas,' January grins at her. 'Have a look at what I've got.'

It's just an old jar. The lid feels rough under Jasmine's fingers and leaves orange marks on her fingertips. She wonders if it tastes like cheese, like the orange marks left by chippies, but the taste is a disappointing metallic.

'What is it?'

'Do you remember when Princess January forgot her name?'

'Yes.'

'Well, it's in here.'

Jasmine looks at the jar. 'It's empty.'

'Oh, it's in there. Just waiting for the right person to open it.'

'Is it me?'

'You can try.'

Jasmine tries to budge the lid with all the strength in her arms, but ends up with nothing but orange-streaked hands, which she promptly wipes on her t-shirt.

'Can you open it, January?'

'Maybe, but it is not for me to do. The spell won't be broken then.'

Jasmine nods. It seems to be the way with spells on princesses; they always need someone else to break them. Jasmine feels sorry for January, who is clearly under a spell. Why else would a princess wear such boring clothes?

Any guilt that January feels about manipulating a small child is forgotten as Jasmine beams at her.

'January, do you think Mae could open it?'

twenty-eight

January is summoned to see Mae. Jasmine, the tiny bailiff, doesn't want to ask January what she's done because she has the same look on her face that her brothers and sisters wear when they are called to their mother.

January is in trouble.

Jasmine squeezes January's hand a little tighter.

Mae sits propped up in bed looking regal and frail at the same time. It is as if, as her body fails her, her spirit has gained a certain freedom. January is unsure Mae's eyes would look as angry if she had time to waste. She desperately wants to run away: the sight of Mae like this is too real for her. She had imagined this, of course, but it was sanitised; a vaseline-lensed vision that would cut away before it became too sad. January denies every urge in her body, pretending that she is staying strong for the child at her side. Jasmine, life brimming out of every pore, seems oblivious to mortality, and January wishes that she could protect her from what will inevitably happen. She could lock Jasmine in a glass bottle keeping her safe from the outside world; keep her innocent. But the only way to be truly protected against Life is to not live it, and January cannot wish that upon Jasmine.

Jasmine lets go of January's hand and settles in the part of the room she has claimed for herself, busying herself with crayons and paper.

January feels anchorless without Jasmine; she longs to retreat into the fantasy they have been creating together. But that would defeat the reason she came here. The reason she waited for Mae to see her. January finally feels something for someone, and she will not let an uncomfortable silence stop her.

'Mae.'

Mae beckons January closer, and January leans in to her. So close that she can hear Mae's breath tearing at the edges as it escapes her lips.

'It's unfair to use a child like that.'

'Hello Pot, my name is Kettle.'

January thinks she sees Mae smile for a second before she turns away and looks at Jasmine. To be that young again, to take a friendship offered as just that; not aware that some people befriend you for other reasons. January wonders if this is the reason that her friendship with Mae is so complicated; they have set up ulterior motives and agendas between them. The things they have shared – the deal, the lessons, the journal – have served to keep them apart, so neither have to admit that they miss each other and just like the other's company.

Their game has grown old, but neither is brave enough to stop it. Perhaps if they had more time they could learn how to just be, but this is not something January can hope for now. All she wants is to be let back in, on whatever terms are on offer.

Mae holds the jar carefully in her hands.

'Do you need me to open it for you?'

Mae looks at January with cold eyes. *Careful girl.*

'It is part of what I owe you, Mae.'

'This is not the story I want.'

'But this is.'

January places the jar on the bedside table to make room for the journal.

'It made compelling reading.'

Mae slowly turns each page. To the layman the writing would seem identical to hers, but Mae can see the discrepancies, the deviations, the deceit.

'If I had known your talent for forgery, we could have spent our time more profitably.'

January's laugh is cut short by Mae's glare.

'This doesn't mean I forgive you. It wasn't just the loss of this.' Mae throws the journal on the bed.

'It was that you had no regard for me or my life. I could have spent the last of my time here, with people that cared about me.'

'I just wanted to learn.'

'Did you? Tell me then, January, what is the most important tool a graphologist has?'

January cannot look Mae in the eye; the fire in them burns her.

'Empathy, January. It is something that I cannot teach; it is something that you cannot learn.'

January places her hand over Mae's. She doesn't know how hard she can squeeze it; at what point the pressure would be too much. 'We could try.'

Time at the Raine house is inverted: January spends her days with Mae and her nights filling her journal with the stories Mae tells or with her feelings, almost too new to acknowledge. January wants to be there for everything, but most mornings she sleeps through the first cup of tea that Cheryl makes.

'You'll make yourself sick. Are you sleeping?'

January stares at her tea before shaking free the sleep that has clouded her head.

'A few hours at night and a couple more when she naps.'

Cheryl shakes her head and tuts.

'Cheryl, you know that this might be the only time …'

'I know, I know. Just eat something; you're beginning to fade away.'

But January has never felt so conspicuous, like the sharp black underline of Mae's headings. Her focus on Mae has defined her: made the borders between her and the world finally real.

Today is a good day: Mae wants to chat; stories about this house and her father.

'I was born into a family of night cart men. My father was a night cart man, as was his father before him. The tradition stretched beyond anyone's memory, back to biblical times.'

'What's a night cart, Mae?'

'Ah, you're too young to remember. Before flush toilets we used a privy outside. The night cart man would deliver a fresh can to your privy and take away the full one.'

January wrinkles her nose and Mae laughs.

'You couldn't see him coming, but you could smell the cart. When I was sixteen I could track my father's progress around town with a sniff. I could sneak out of the house to the cinema and never get caught.'

Mae's words rasp as her throat dries, and January pours her a glass of water.

'I was allowed to help my father only once. I sat close to him on the cart listening to the clip-clop of our horse, Blackie. I tried my best not to yawn, not to betray the tiredness I felt being up past my bedtime. My father would take the full cans and I would replace them with the new. It had all been going well until we reached the privy of a friend of mine, Millie. I just couldn't get the tin into place, but I was determined not to ask my father for help. I wanted so much for him to be proud of me. So I got underneath and pulled, and at that precise moment I heard Millie's sigh as she relieved herself all over me. She had been in the privy when my father arrived so she decided to hold on, waiting until he had gone. He had gone all right, but I hadn't! I screamed, which frightened poor Millie to death, and then she screamed. My father rushed around and picked me up, holding me an arm's length away as he took me back to the cart. Poor Millie; I bet she jumped right out of her skin.'

'A good place to shit yourself though.'

Mae throws her head back and laughs.

'So that ended my short-lived career as a night cart man.'

'But how did you become a graphologist?'

'It was because of a promise that my father had to keep. One of the two things my mother left me when she died.'

'And the other?'

'She left me wanting more, and now, dear January, I gift it to you.'

Mae settles back in the bed and is soon asleep. January is not far behind as she twists herself into the chair beside Mae's bed.

On bad days, Mae still wants to chat, but her stories turn to mortality. She tells them with a fever that seems to consume her body. All that January can offer in comfort is a damp facecloth and her attention.

'My father died of a broken heart. I had been careless with him, so wrapped in my own life that I couldn't see that he was an integral part of it. When I left, I took it for granted that he would be there when I got back. I thought he'd live forever.'

Mae seems lucid, although her brow is sweaty.

'We only had each other. He sent me away for a better life, but I will always be the daughter of a night cart man. He died alone in the dark, slumped in his cart. Blackie, his horse, kept plodding on, keeping his steady rhythm as my father lost his.'

January wipes the tears from Mae's eyes, unsure if they're from the pain of her memory or of her body. Mae clutches January's hand tighter, and smiles. That's how they work best, January and Mae. Leaving what is unsaid hanging between them as obvious as the writing they study; they live between the lines.

Jasmine draws Mae in the bed and January beside her. She draws until her mother knocks softly on the door to collect her for dinner. She pleads with her mother to let her stay, but Cheryl silences her with a shake of the head, and promises of tomorrow, tomorrow.

Jasmine wants to tell her mother all about what happened, but she can't remember the details at all. Jasmine wishes she knew more than how to write her name, and then she could tell her mother the story. Instead she shows her mother the last picture she drew. Two women smiling, their hands linked.

January stays in Mae's room far beyond exhaustion, scared that if she leaves she'll miss something. She just wants to remember everything about Mae, even this: she wants to remember them like this.

Mae coughs, and January winces and gives her hand a squeeze. Mae's hand is warm and soft against her skin: each touch feels like a new sensation since she has liberated her hands from their gloves. A moment passes before either of them realises that this simple gesture no longer feels awkward. Somehow, without either of them noticing, this has become natural.

'Go to bed. I'm not dead yet. I'll see you in the morning.'

But Mae lies.

January wakes to rain on the iron roof, the rat-a-tat-tat tapping her awake. The house has a chill unusual for this time of year; the southerly that bought the rain must have brought the cold too. Some time in the night the fire in the stove had gone out, and January tries to resuscitate it with wood wet from the rain. She tries two, three times before she gives up to wait for Cheryl to light it when she gets in.

Mae will have to wait for her tea. January opens Mae's door to tell her, but Mae is still asleep. January touches Mae's hand and cheek; the chill in the air is contagious. She hugs her arms around herself as she sinks to the floor.

'Morning. January? Jas, go wake January while I light the fire.'

Cheryl opens the range. It looks like someone has already tried to light it. Strange. Maybe they felt the southerly more keenly up here last night.

'Mummy, she's not in her room.'

Cheryl tries to hide her concern from her daughter. 'You stay here Jas, I'll just check on Mae.'

Cheryl walks to Mae's room and knocks lightly on the door before pushing it open.

'She's gone.'

January is on the floor dressed only in a t-shirt and the gumboots that live by the back door, hugging her knees.

'I couldn't get the fire going.' January is shivering but she doesn't notice. 'Her tea is going to be late.'

Cheryl wraps the quilt from Mae's bed around January.

'No. Mae will get cold …'

'January …'

'No! She'll get cold.'

January takes the quilt from around her and tucks it back around Mae. 'I should have been here.'

Cheryl hugs her; the warmth of her body makes January's numb fingers pulse.

'I should have been here.'

Mae has made and paid for most of the arrangements, but there are still the little things, the important things, to decide. An outfit Mae would like (a dress, red floral, that she had tucked away for a special occasion); the lipstick she preferred (also red but with a little brown in it); how she preferred her hair set. Although Cheryl knows all of these things intimately she always defers to January.

Isn't that right, January?

What do you think, January?

I think Mae would have liked that, don't you, January?

January nods and helps where she can, but she feels like the whole world should stop: just until she catches her breath again.

People have been stopping by the house, dropping off casseroles and condolences. When Mae comes back from the funeral parlour, they drop by the sitting room to pay their respects. Cheryl plays hostess for them, making tea and offering biscuits, but January finds it far too draining to talk with them.

When the call comes from Mae's lawyer, January is happy to drive down to Wellington, if only for a few hours' peace.

She stops by the hotel when she arrives back later. 'I need a drink, Jimmy.'

'You and me both,' Jimmy pours two glasses of whiskey, neat. 'You and me both.'

January's room has been locked all morning. Jasmine knocks, but there is no answer. The house smells good: her mother has cleaned everything and the doors are flung open. Cakes and savouries cool on the table, and no one dares to nick any of them. Jasmine's dress scratches her neck and feels tight across her chest. She wanders into Mae's room, as empty as the jar January had brought with her. A couple of days ago, January finally opened it. Jasmine had been expecting something more to happen. But they just leaned closer together and whispered, Mae falling back and smiling as January hurriedly put the lid back on. Jasmine hasn't seen Mae since, although she knows where Mae is.

Jasmine wonders if Mae would protect her from the other ghosts in the sitting room if she went in for a visit. She doesn't want to go in by herself.

'Mum ...'

'Jas, I'm busy. Go outside for a while.'

Jasmine mopes outside. She can't do anything fun because she isn't allowed to get her dress dirty. She finds a bit of wood and climbs up it to peek in January's window. January hasn't changed her clothes for days. She just stares straight ahead, the lights still on in her room like she doesn't realise it is day.

That's when Jasmine hears Cat. She moves the wood aside and sees Cat's eyes glowing under the house. She puts her hand in the gap, and Cat moves back. Jasmine moves a little closer, and Cat backs off. Before she knows it, Jasmine is under the house, crawling after Cat.

She traipses dirt along the hallway just cleaned this morning, holding Cat to her chest, which will be covered in the fur that Cat has shed in fright. She walks into the sitting room with Cat.

'Look who's come for a visit, Mae.'

It was a small service really. January thought that she, Cheryl and Jasmine were the only ones that knew Mae and the rest of the people were neck-craners just there to know what was going on. Until one by one they offered their condolences and their stories of Mae; little pieces of her story that could not be found in the pages of her journal. Memories of friendships with parents and later their children, photographs of Mae in faded colour – she was never as sharp as when she was in black and white. January is unsure if she really knew Mae at all – she just has a fraction of her caught on paper. The edited, rewritten Mae, carefully and thoughtfully constructed. She just knew the broad strokes of most people; perhaps, in time, graphology would give her shading. But to really know someone, the details that make a person real and rounded, you have to have lived with them. The talks which seemed such a waste of time to January before, the way Mae liked her porridge in the morning, the expression on her face when she got a card in the mail: these things are just as important, maybe even more so, than the lessons Mae left in her journal.

January sits numb at the kitchen table in the fading afternoon sun. She has no idea how long she has been there. She unconsciously sips the tea that has been silently placed at her elbow. It coats her tongue, the bittersweet liquid bringing her back around to reality.

'Thank you.' January can finally thank Cheryl; she has been bustling around the kitchen making tea and dinner for January, who doesn't realise she hasn't eaten all day.

January is amazed at Cheryl's resilience; a few hours ago she grieved openly for a woman she knew all her life. Large tears rolled down her face while January could hardly muster a frown. She envied Cheryl then; her tears were allowed to flow freely, while January's festered within her, knotting her stomach and making her head ache. Cheryl's grief was exorcised immediately; her tears stopped as soon as she washed the soil from her hands.

January wishes she could cry. Wishes she could feel anything but the aching emptiness.

'I had better go. There's a casserole in the oven. Will you be all right?'

January nods and then surprises herself and Cheryl when she pulls Cheryl to her. Cheryl's strong arms grip her, and a small sigh of breath is forced out of her mouth. Cheryl mistakes it for a sob, and begins to weep once more. January's cheeks are finally wet; a borrowed approximation of sorrow provided by Cheryl's tears. January wishes her own eyes would sting. She wishes she could prove that she loved Mae too.

She pulls away from Cheryl and retrieves a small tin that Mae had given her strict instructions to deliver.

'She wanted me to give you this.' January hands Cheryl the tin of sweets, and a broad white smile breaks Cheryl's tears. She smiles as her eyes turn heavenward, her hand clasped to her lips.

If she's so excited about that, wait till she finds out that Mae left her the house.

The car is already packed when Cheryl and Jasmine arrive to see January off. Cat meows, trapped in her cage in the car, and Jasmine lets herself into the car to pat her.

'You don't have to go yet; stay as long as you need to.'

'I have things to do at home; besides, if I stay much longer I'll have to start paying you rent.'

Cheryl looks beyond January to the house that she has cleaned all of her adult life. She knows every corner of that place, but had never imagined it to be hers.

'She didn't have to. I didn't expect anything for looking after her.'

'Mae gave it to you for purely selfish reasons. She wanted someone who loved the place, who would look after it.'

'Like you would sell it.'

January just shrugs and winks at Cheryl.

'What are you going to do with it?'

'I don't know. I never expected to own anything, y'know? I think it's going to take a while to sink in. But I think we could be happy here. And of course you're welcome to stay, January; I can just kick the kids into the sitting room.'

Cheryl gives January a quick hug, and nods to her daughter in the back seat.

'I think you've got company.'

January gets in the car and starts the engine. She looks at Jasmine in the rear view mirror.

'Where to, Ma'am?'

Jasmine giggles, and January turns around in her seat, hugging the back of it as if she is holding on for dear life.

'Are you going to miss me, January?'

'Maybe. Are you going to miss me?'

'Nope.'

'Well, thanks a lot.'

'I'm coming with you. I want to know the end of the story.'

'You know what they say about cats and curiosity …'

Jasmine looks puzzled as she pats Cat. January laughs a little at her expense.

'Ask your mother.'

'I miss Mae, January.'

'Me too.'

'Will you come back and visit?'

January hugs Jasmine through the gap in the front seats. 'Of course I will.'

January toots and waves to Cheryl and Jasmine as she drives off.

She stops in at the hotel on her way out, and Jimmy pulls down a bottle of whiskey from the shelf.

'No thanks, Jimmy, I'd better not. Driving home.'

Jimmy hugs her. 'Are you sure you're not leaving it?'

'I've got to go, Cat's in the car ...'

'January ...' she turns around as he calls. 'Don't be a stranger.'

She smiles and walks out the door.

The cottage seems impossibly the same. January opens the gate and the door as she always does. She stands in the hall for a minute, still clutching Mae's suitcase, surveying her domain. It is everything she ever wanted: a place of her own, a home; but now it feels empty.

It is not until the journal lies on her bed that January can finally acknowledge the reality. Mae is not coming back. She cries in a heap on the bed. Cat crawls into her arms to comfort her, and licks away her tears.

I'll take care of you now.

In the confusion of her grief, January is unsure if Cat has read her mind or if January has read Cat's.

She cries herself to sleep between the two things that mattered most to Mae. January hopes she was at least a poor third. But something inside her tells her she was that, and more, otherwise Mae would have never entrusted her with her treasures.

twenty-nine

The sun is acutely aware that it is the day after the night before: it filters its morning light through gauzy clouds as the city nurses its hangover. More than one person's resolution this morning will be to never drink again, but this promise will easily be broken this evening as the smell of barbeque hangs in the air, and hair of the dog makes the queasiness subside.

The sunlight streams into the lounge of a small, one-bedroom flat in the cheap part of the inner city. Not because the occupant is an early riser, but because she forgot to close the curtains before she went out last night.

There has been no movement in the flat since the door opened in the early hours of the morning; the only evidence of life is the trail of clothes that lead from the door to the bedroom and the light snores from the bed.

Fashion magazines lie open on the table; pages have been ripped out and the two-dimensional models – are there any other kind? – sit next to a scalpel awaiting their final surgery. Glue, pens and glitter will complete their transformation on the new board – started yesterday and to be finished today, in the New Year. It is a resolution, a physical manifestation of a wish and a signpost: because this year will be different. The word 'friendship' is written in block letters in the middle of the board, and already a few images are crowding the edges. This year the friendship that is sought will be true. There is no room for toxic people; people who cannot or will not honour the woman that she is. But already a picture reminding her of January's sardonic smile has been glued down and another so like her eyebrow arch is stuck on the bottom of the board – the rest of the face cut off like she is behind a cubicle wall and a pair of coffee cups sit cradled between the 'i' and 'd' of friend. It has been a struggle to get this far: this board just doesn't want to be made. Magazines have been searched again and again for the right images; the lettering has been done by hand because she couldn't find the word. She had considered cutting up letters like they do in ransom notes, but had thought the universe might misinterpret her intention; she doesn't want a friend she has to cajole to talk to her.

The board will eventually end up on her bedroom wall, placed at just the right height so that she will see it every morning. It will replace the 'boyfriend' board that is hastily hidden every time he stays over. On those nights the board jostles for room with its siblings in her wardrobe; she keeps them all because she is not certain what to do with them, superstitious that if she gets rid of them then the bounty they have brought will disappear from her life.

A screwed-up piece of paper on the corner of the table is too tempting for Chairman Meow. His paw stabs at it until it falls to the ground. He bats it between his paws for a while before he has to attend to an emergency fur snarl. Finally presentable, he begins his patrol sitting on the back of the couch, his eyes slits in the sunlight. Later he will follow the sun around to the back and watch out the bedroom window until dinner time. From his post he can see the street, the birds and the buses as they go past, the tom next door sneaking around. From his post he can see someone walking up the path to the front door.

Alice hits her alarm clock twice, but the ringing doesn't stop. Perhaps it is another hangover from last night: the eighties music was turned up so loud that she thought it was the sound that moved her and not her own limbs.

The doorbell.

Part of Alice screams at her to stay in bed, to just ignore it; it is probably Mormons or Witnesses anyway, and she'll have to politely nod and tell them that she already has a non-denominational path. Which, to them, means a path straight to hell and repeat visits for Alice. Or it could be him, impatient to see her again, although they only parted a couple of hours ago. Perhaps she *should* give him the key she has cut and hidden in her drawer, ready for the 'right time'. The books she has read say it is too soon; that she might scare him off. They also say that she shouldn't be too available; that people will respect her more if she isn't always there for them. But her legs don't listen to reason, and they are already on their way to the door. Chairman Meow does his best to trip her up on the way, protesting about the lack of breakfast this morning. All the while the doorbell rings and rings. It would be just her luck if she opened the door to no one; whoever it was too impatient to wait. Alice opens the door to find the unexpected on her doorstep.

'January?'

'Happy New Year, Alice.'

'I haven't heard from you in weeks. What are you doing here?'

'I just wanted to say ...'

'What? What could you possibly say that would interest me, January?'

'I'm ... sorry?'

Alice is not sure if it is an apology, or if January simply cannot believe what she has heard.

'I've been thinking a lot. Here.'

January hands Alice a paper cup of coffee. Alice pops the lid off and the aroma lifts her smile.

'I owe you one.'

'Just the one?'

'It's a start.'

The start of what? Alice thinks of the vision board drying in her lounge, and wonders if January is the missing piece she's been looking for. This year was supposed to be about new beginnings; not reverting back to bad habits. Alice doesn't want to be that person any more; she can't support January any longer.

'Thanks for the coffee.'

Alice tries to close the door but it is stopped by January's hand.

'Look, I know I haven't been the best ... well, anything really. I just wanted ... I just hoped ... Friends?'

Be careful what you wish for, eh Alice?

Chairman Meow sits between them. His rasping mew, like that of a pack-a-day smoker, is ignored. Alice finally breaks the silence.

'Come in.'

January stands in the hall, unsure of which direction she should take, before Alice guides her way.

'Excuse the mess,' Alice says as she picks up clothes from the ground. 'It was a bit of a late one.'

She disappears with an armful of clothes, and January wanders around the room looking at Alice's collection of things as if they are clues. She sees a collection of fashion magazines with pages ripped out and cut into pieces, some of which have been stuck to a board.

'It's a hobby of mine, I guess. Power of positive thinking. You probably think it's stupid.'

'I like it, Alice.'

January traces the word 'friendship'. How could she have misread Alice, when her intentions have always been plain? She blinks her eyes rapidly, trying to stave off the tears. January's relationship with two women rendered in ten hot pink letters: Alice, open, honest and friendly, wanting just a friend; and Mae, the woman who taught her to see that. January had always thought of her life as a straight line, ruled across in HB pencil, but lately it is like each event is linked, that she rounds back to the past before springing to the future like she is following the gentle curve of a well-formed letter. January lets her tears go and they roll down her cheek onto the board, blurring the letters. She fights the habits of the past: the urge to run, or to dismiss her emotions with sarcasm. She had once thought Alice was foolish and stupid to let herself be so ... it is a struggle for January to be how Alice is naturally: open and real.

'Are you all right, Jan?'

January smiles, and like everything she does it is a contradiction. She weeps as though her heart is broken, but her smile is full of ... Alice can't put her finger on the word. Joy? Alice has never thought of January as joyful. But people can surprise you, and January does it again with her answer:

'Yes.'

acknowledgements

The author is grateful for the support of Renée, Phillip Mann, whānau and friends and the Randell Cottage Creative New Zealand Residency.

The author acknowledges the following sources used in researching graphology: *Encyclopedia of the Written Word: A Lexicon for Graphology and Other Aspects of Writing*, written and compiled by Klara G Roman and edited by Rose Wolfson and Maurice Edwards; *Handwriting: A Key to Personality* by Klara G Roman; and *Applied Graphology* by A J Smith.